the
lonely
crowd

the lonely crowd

Editing & Design John Lavin

Cover Photo John Lavin

Online Fiction Editor Matthew David Scott

ISBN 978-1-9164987-7-8

Please direct all initial enquiries to johnlavin@thelonelycrowd.org

Visit our website for exclusive online content
www.thelonelycrowd.org

Follow us on blusky @thelonelycrowd.bsky.social, *x at*
twitter.com/thelonelypress, *Instagram* thelonelycrowdpressltd
& Facebook The Lonely Crowd

This issue is dedicated to our dear friend

Chris Cornwell R.I.P.

Contents

issue fourteen

Introduction
John Lavin

This fourteenth edition of The Lonely Crowd carries with it the weight of loss. Our dear friend and collaborator, Christopher Cornwell, passed away earlier this year at a youthful age that is still difficult to comprehend. Longstanding readers of this publication will know that Chris appeared in several early issues before going on to guest edit the poetry section in Issue Seven. It was around this time that we published his virtuoso debut collection, *Ergasy*, a book that made good on Chris' editorial declaration that 'Language must become non-normative. Become extraordinary.'

We were thrilled that John Goodby, the world-renowned authority on Dylan Thomas, agreed to write an introduction, declaring *Ergasy*: 'a ridiculously quotable book, full of phrases that will live with you'. Professor Goodby contributes 'Early Doors' to this volume; a necessarily bittersweet but nevertheless joyful poem in memory of his friendship with Chris.

Chris was a huge inspiration to me when I first met him at Lampeter University in 2009. I had never really met anyone at that time who loved to talk about literature as much as I did. After a short while, I quickly realised that although Chris was ten years younger than me, he knew a great deal more about literature than I did. He became a constant source of advice while I began The Lampeter Review before becoming a vital presence when I later founded The Lonely Crowd. It is no exaggeration to say that his literary ability and his questioning, excoriating intellect influenced this publication to an unquantifiable extent. Asides from the fact that I loved him dearly, it is for this reason that Issue Fourteen is dedicated to Christopher Cornwell.

Three Poems
Medbh McGuckian

Ave Maria Stanzas

What is poetry? The feeling of a former world and future one.
Organic life is unceasingly occupied with connecting to new forms
those elements liberated by death.

She has her country marks in her forehead
and a firebrand in one of her breasts.
A stab of a knife almost into the small of her back,
a mark of a whip on one eye.

I send her my last night's dream,
of eighty seasoned negroes, where Broad street
meets White street. Night is a religious
concern, like rust in overnight dew.

Though I am no great admirer of tangible
religions, I purchased a shilling's worth
of salvation, rushing towards some newly
blessed water in a lidded landscape

or a girl's harp bequeathed unquenchingly.
The week of his death, his angel was dead,
angels can sprain their wings or cough
in their wingsuits at the limitations of dawn.

Words are never someone, never completely
something. Life has another meaning than to be
lived: full ruby moon lost again, so overboughed
a burst lake, robin with white moth.

The border tore through her thin ghost
that shreds be not the secret's fate.
Earth is, after all, one of the major characters,
the moon insists, through me, through me,

ribbed blue. The most built windows in
long strips ascend to the inside of a cloud,
a cloud approaches, pauses, settles
in a roof a clouds, so clear my eyes.

The clock that ticks once every year
is a word that is every vowel at once.
Was all that floral painting done
by the angels in vain? Little was the fault

of the branching tresses. Many of the watchers
knew well enough that death was in charge
of the production. Memories of the future
are remembering differently, remembering again.

The slow cancellation of the future,
of connections between fields, suppressing
all the emptiness of the body, its houseness.
I place my hand like a shell on a lover's face.

How do you imitate a building, just pushed
a little further, like bones without a skeleton,
endless house shadow in a very new street
as though no new dust could be added to it.

Space stands so still it gathers dust like a coat
of sleep. The unearthed dust of an interior that
refuses dust, throws time into the outside, asleep
within the once upon a time of the see-through butterfly.

Walking with the Weather

A grey light with a gossamer tinge
Through his eyes. Those diaphanous
Hands, on the dawn which follows
The midnight after a death.
Their nearness lent a new weight
To the interlocking between angels,
Blackmarket lemons on a forest day
When I cottoned on to this and ruled
The winter, in a sheltered river whose
Mouth is hidden, since death itself is
After all an angel.

In Milton angels were a mirror
Of God's thoughts, though they themselves
May not be eternal, they caused
The fall of one third of the stars.
Our rage for angelic protection softens
The olive wood angels, the answering
Angel by way of dreamfast. Each
Of our souls is sown in a star, or stored
Away in the planets by the angel
Christ, the earth of the soul is a climate
That secretes its own light.

Our shallower companion, Time, is an
Envious shadow, plaiting hair that looks
Like air, our cloudy child of black
Summer fires. You have to rely on moonlight,
The best red of self-willed land with its
Occasional outbursts of willow, the creeping
Advent of the river's personhood, the ld
Weather sensations like a yellow archangel,
A variant of seasonal radiance. If words

Were said but not recorded, the expected
Weather is wrong.

When we weather a place we have memories
Of winds and mid-green leaves - and not just
Any weather. Earth is always on the move,
Using weather events and weather ways, child-
Weather, slow–walking moments outside the storm.
We cannot know the weather from the outside,
Skin should be rethought, weather happens to us,
More than human weather, the presence of rain
Is the geography closest in. I look at
The weather three times a day, hoping for clear
Airturbulence.

Hoping it will show us some mercy. We not only
Touch a breeze, we transform water, you feel
Nothing but it melts. A hard wind adds
A layer of meaning to our thinking weather,
To make weather useful to all the weather
It suffers. Another handful of summers with
The rate of meadow loss, as shade trees flex
At how we weather the world. Beyond the
Footprint of the bypass is an alpine clarity
From Celsius days in January and the dump
Of the atmosphere.

Through ghost forests a new tree is a soft promise
Of shiny white lithium, out into the shared sky.
It was going to be curtains for our country,
Some might ask what such dismantling
Is worth, we're talking about a long time ago.
To be partially buried, by air vacating a room,
Or gardens of piano-absorbent foliage,
Each key into your teetering countryside

Frees the cloud storage in the computer
That will fully understand it, as out as one can
Imagine, without killing trees.

So the Lost Year Ends

The road is even more secretive
From the church-shaped well to a sky
Burnt white by noon, by moon.
Who forced me to dream about this
Languid angel, whose dreams threaten the world?

She goes to her icy bed, I would have
Hurried to her voice. Our time here
Is limited as the shade, on such and such
A day. I do not want these half-filled
Masks, or her purely album verses.

Most of the cafes were shut, under flimsy
Brown trees in a sheared meadow,
Brown cloud swelled deeper than the ear.
The dead can do no wrong, except try to be
Younger, by several centuries.

Snow brought the dead houses back to life,
In the evacuated villages. I would cry
Because I had cried, each time I was brought
Back by some slight noise in the house,
Prepared to see less of her this winter.

There is a third wind which loves islands,
We had to sit in splendid isolation or end
By being more or less compromised demi-
Vierges. I felt the time with my fingers,
The clocks deepening into autumn.

They are all away somewhere, freeing
The country. Once I belonged here,
To the sad roads. No winter is ever easy,
Sunset is an intellectual experience, little
By little the streets begin to people themselves
Once more, as I stand waiting for the stars to begin.

Mature People
Mary Morrissy

When Olivia reaches her destination there's a canvas tent outside where she has to show her card to an official. It reminds her of images she's seen on TV of al-fresco voting in some hot country where the people are eager for everyday democracy. She likes the primitive simplicity of it – the tent, well really an awning on stilts, and the atmosphere of doughty war-time solidarity, as the steward jokes with her about the weather. It's July but it's the same grey, he says. He ushers her into a huge basketball arena with a polished wooden floor. She has to register first at a row of tables where staff with lanyards sit in Perspex boxes in front of screens. The first question she's asked is her date of birth. She overhears the man beside her give his – it's identical to Olivia's, and she wants to say 'snap!' or 'what are the odds?' Then she realises how stupid she is. Everyone here is the same vintage – that's the whole point.

The steward at the start of the roped walkway leading to the vaccination stalls is standing with her back to Olivia, where a number of people are queueing. She's a heavy-set young woman and something about her shape looks familiar. These days Olivia finds it harder and harder to 'see' people in all the hazard gear. When the steward turns, she's wearing a pair of black-framed spectacles, large as goggles. She holds her hand up policing the air between them.

'Marcella?'

'Liv?' Marcella says peering, then flaps her hands. 'Oh, it must be my new glasses!'

Olivia doesn't know if she means that she can't see properly or that they've transformed her appearance. Either way, Olivia thinks, the glasses have nothing to do with it. It's the estrangement that has overtaken the world since they last met that has made them unsure of one another.

'How *are* you?' Olivia asks.

Marcella shrugs. 'You know.'
'Still writing?'

*

She'd met Marcella on a writing masters in Trinity College, although they called it something posher. An MPhil. It had never made Olivia feel in the slightest philosophical. When she started the course, in fact, she'd been feeling strangely bereft. Bernard had just left on his retirement trip to China. It was the first time they'd been parted for any significant period of time in 40 years. Imagine! He'd wanted her to come with him but she'd refused.

'I have my own plans, thank you very much!' she said while thinking *we are not joined at the hip.*

They were like an old married couple. An old married couple without the sex. Or maybe that *was* the definition of an old married couple; she wouldn't know.

The difference was that she and Bernard had never been intimate. Not in that way.

Once they came of age, Olivia's sons refused to believe it.

'Right, yeah!' Charlie said. He's 20, a tousle-haired beanpole, cheeky and forthright, and so like his long-vanished father that sometimes Olivia has to turn away from him out of fright. Fright and memory. For Charlie and Mal, Bernard has always been Uncle Ber. They wouldn't have objected to him as a substitute father. He'd have been a hell of a lot better than some of the specimens she did go out with over the years. But, at least, Olivia had had enough sense not to move any of them in. So Bernard remained the only feasible candidate, as far as the boys were concerned, although they were convinced that Uncle Ber was a closeted gay. In their circular thinking, it was the only logical explanation for why she and Bernard hadn't 'hooked up'.

The writing course was held in a Georgian terrace of houses fronting on to Westland Row, but covered in at the back – the part that faced the campus – by a glassed-in atrium. Inside it felt like a greenhouse and made the students streaming by in droves seem like rare botanical plants who needed this glaring dry heat to sprout. This architectural incorporation meant the backs of the houses that used to be external were interior walls now. That was how Olivia felt like most of the time while she was in Trinity – like someone whose mottled insides were on display.

The workshop room was on an upper floor. There were two long windows that partitioned the skies of several seasons into four takeaway portions. The students sat around the edges of the room in a U-formation. There was a large empty space in the centre that looked like a bull-ring waiting for Hemingway. Olivia remembered reading somewhere that workshops were the blood sports of the literary world. As she sat there on her first day with her eager new writing notebooks and plastic folders, she felt very old and very prominent. If only there had been one other older person. But no, she told herself firmly, it was better this way; she wouldn't be part of some oldies' ghetto.

First item of business was appointing the class reps. Really? After 40 years as a council clerk and an active union member, Olivia thought she was done with tedious business like this. This was, at last, her me-time.

'Volunteers?' the lecturer asked testily.

He was Theo Bender, a visiting Scandi writer, who spoke English with dental precision. He was a very tall young man in his 30s with Nordic blond hair and a stone-coloured ski jumper with a rust-coloured pattern scattered across the shoulders. He wore jeans and hiking boots and had the scrubbed complexion of someone who had trudged directly from the Arctic to be with them. (Olivia was disappointed to learn that everyone teaching her was going to be younger than her. She wanted white-haired men in academic gowns, she realised, or if they were going to be younger, someone rakish and disreputable like Michael Caine in *Educating Rita*.)

'Anyone?'

This in bureaucratic terms was the equivalent to a drowning person calling 'help, help' as he goes down for the third time.

'Would one of the mature people volunteer?' Theo said, looking directly at her. Technically, she wasn't the only mature student – you only had to be 23 to qualify – but she was the only one who looked it.

'Come, come, it is not a chair on the UN security council. It is a simple job dealing with people's complaints.'

Oh well, Olivia thought, I can do that.

She looked around the group. Young hip folk who, fashion-wise, looked like refugees from her own disreputable youth – the young men with beards, in collarless shirts, and ripped jeans. The girls were sculpted into leggings (another throwback for Olivia; she'd belonged to the first leggings generation) or wore outsize floral dresses or tiny denim shorts. How on earth could she represent them?

'Do you really want someone as old as your mother?' she asked and then silently corrected herself – as your granny, more like.

They all laughed, more out of nervousness than anything else. They didn't find her self-deprecating humour funny, she could see; time was when that would have appealed. Now, it sounded like special pleading.

'So, you will do it? Yes?' Theo Bender said.

*

Olivia's first misconception was not realising how much she'd be expected to write. How foolish that sounded in retrospect. She'd written confessional poetry secretly in her 20s – an unhappy marriage will do that to you – but having spent a lifetime in between reading voraciously for escape, she wanted to master the more muscular world of fiction now. Even so, she realised early on that her notion of writing as something languid and elective, was not what was on offer here. This was closer to a spinning session at the gym. They were expected to cough up 500 words at a moment's notice and Olivia was aghast at how mechanical it all was, as if they were wind-up toys that could only be set in motion by a series of prompts. Although, left to her own devices, Olivia would probably have been left chewing her pencil end. Metaphorically, that is. Everything, she learned, was a metaphor.

Ideas were not her strong suit, though she had a certain fluidity from a lifetime of writing memos and fictional sick notes for her boys. *Malcolm is feeling bilious* (a word she'd always wanted to use) *this morning after a sea journey; Charlie has the mumps* (which he had five times in all) *and must be quarantined.* But those first weeks, their practice, as it was grandly called, reminded her of those pasta machines, where you fed a fat piece of dough in one end and it came out in thin strings at the other.

The young people didn't seem to mind. But then it wasn't 40 years since they'd last been in a classroom. She saw the hesitation when classes ended and the young ones were drifting off for coffee unsure of whether to ask her along. They belonged to the generation who didn't want to exclude anybody, but they didn't want an elderly gooseberry for company either. She understood their dilemma but she was determined never to exclude herself either. She wanted the full university experience so she accepted all invites – to poetry readings from Fliss and Emer, and to pub quizzes by Dermot and Carl who needed someone for the vintage trivia questions.

Carl was a beautiful, bald, black American (he told her he had Cuban heritage) who wore John Lennon glasses and was still the right side of 40. He could recite Yeats at the drop of a hat. His party piece was 'To A Friend Whose Work Has Come to Nothing'. Olivia had to train herself to stop sizing him up. Really! You're a 60-year-old woman, stop! Not only is your lust sexist, it's probably racist too. Dermot, on the other hand, was a bashful 21-year-old, so thin he was almost concave. Marmalade-haired, pale, given to furious smoking which made his breath smell terrible. Olivia was working up to telling him but never did. The last thing she wanted was to come off as motherly.

*

'Well,' Marcella says 'I *was* writing a speculative historical novel about Jane Eyre's cousin, John Reid. . .'

Olivia doesn't hear the rest of the sentence. She doesn't hear the past tense in Marcella's account, because she's awestruck by the girl's inventiveness. All of those young people, she remembered, were fizzing with ideas. That's why she gave up. That's what she told herself. She just didn't have the agility of mind.

'I'm back in my parents' place,' Marcella adds, nodding glumly.

Olivia recognises the grim resignation of an adult child sent back to the creche. Her Mal had been living an independent life in a shared house before all this. Now he was working from home in the back bedroom.

'And are you getting paid?' she asks.

'For writing?' Marcella says and snorts with laughter behind her mask.

'No,' Olivia says, 'for this?'

'Oh no, this is a volunteering position. Gets me out of the house.' Olivia thinks she can detect a smile in this.

'And are you?'

'Am I what?'

'Still writing?'

'Oh no,' Olivia says, 'No, I knew when I was beaten.'

She was sure Marcella blushed behind all the paraphernalia.

'Look, Liv . . .' Marcella began. This time it was Olivia who raised her hand.

'It's fine, Marcella, I'm fine with it. It's not your fault.'

Marcella hung her head and kicked at the ground.

Trying to change the mood, Olivia inquired: 'How's Jamie?'

*

She, Jamie and Marcella were put into a reading group together early in the first semester. They were in their mid-twenties, same age as her boys, so Olivia felt in familiar territory although soon she realised the gaps in her knowledge. Jamie and Marcella hung around together all the time but they were not a couple. Or at least not a declared couple which seemed to be regarded as the worst possible condition.

Jamie was neat, clean-shaven. He had a short back and sides and a sharp way of dressing. He wore natty waistcoats and dicky bows with pink or lilac jeans. His shirts were always pressed. Olivia presumed he was gay. He was one of the few who made physical contact with her; he would tap her forearm with his slender fingers when he wanted to make a point. He'd greet her with a comradely arm around her shoulder. He had a light touch.

She liked his intelligence, which was cool and methodical. He could quote whole paragraphs of other writers' wisdom, many of them people Olivia had never heard of. He seemed steeped in this world she had only dipped her toe into. She remembered what he said about Don de Lillo's Underworld. "It's a big baggy monster He tries like Joyce to squeeze the whole world into it. But shouldn't it be more organized?"

'You mean slimmer,' Marcella said.

'Is it even a novel?'

'Do we have to define it?' Olivia asked.

It was a surprise to her to find she didn't have fixed opinions about the fiction they'd been assigned. She realised how she'd been reading like a child, just gobbling it up. Usually, she found herself silent as Jamie and Marcella batted ideas back and forth.

'I say yes,' Jamie said.

'And I say no!' Marcella said hotly.

'Isn't she great?' Jamie would say after one of these declarations.

Marcella never batted away his compliments as Olivia would have done at that age. She allowed them, even though her default mode was slightly scathing. A curled lip under a nest of tangled tawny hair, and clothes designed to dispel attention. Ungainly dungarees, plaid pinafores. Olivia longed to take her in hand, but she resisted. She was finished being parental. Anyway, she detected something condescending about the way Jamie talked at her, like he was patting a small pet dog on the head. But Olivia liked Jamie too much to pursue that line of thinking

Maybe it was watching him and Marcella together, but in the early weeks of the first term at Trinity, she found herself thinking a lot about Bernard and their history. They had been work colleagues for over 30 years; she knew no one else as long. She'd often toyed with the idea of them as a couple – on certain conditions. If he'd lose a few pounds, if he'd be more manly, grow a pair, she would think to herself, as Bernard danced around her. But even in that she was conflicted. Were he to turn into George Clooney overnight, wouldn't her answer still be no? What she valued about him was his discretion, which she derided as pussyfooting when she didn't want to acknowledge that it was borne out of his feelings for her. His devotion had become her guilty and sustaining pleasure, particularly during those years when the boys were young and there was no one else even remotely interested in her.

She remembered Bernard gratefully from those years – wearing the silly paper crowns for Christmas dinner, making a fool of himself at the watersports centre, rolling and tumbling down water slides with the boys because Olivia couldn't swim. Christ, he even babysat when she was going out on dates. Sometimes she'd found herself irritated by the devotion he would never act on. It made her cruel as if he was the faithful dog who could be kicked and not react.

Really, she could be a right bitch.

Even when she imagined herself and Bernard together, all she could see were the deficits. Wouldn't it be 'settling' at this stage? Settling for less. Then there was his inexperience. What in the world would she do with him? What would it be like being his sexual teacher? On the other hand, she'd be free to mould him into whatever she wanted. Trouble was she didn't know what she wanted because she'd never had it and that was a kind of inexperience too, wasn't it?

She'd even thought of suggesting a white marriage to him. Isn't that what they call it? Like that elderly gentleman she read about who married his male carer to ensure property succession, though neither of them was gay. She and Bernard could grow old together. Would that be so bad? But if it worked, would it remind them of all the wasted time, when they could have been together and weren't? And if it didn't work, what then?

*

'Jamie?' Marcella says. 'Haven't seen him since we left college. Lockdown, you know.'

She's effecting vagueness, but Olivia doesn't believe her. She wonders if that has to do with the mask. Isn't that why people wore masks in the past – to hide behind, to dissemble?

'I think he was planning to teach English in South Korea, but don't know if he ever made it.'

'But you're still in touch, right?' Olivia persists.

Marcella says nothing. Olivia is about to change the subject again when Marcella adds with a strangled sob. 'No. We're not talking.'

'Oh why? What's happened?'

'You were right about him, Liv. He broke my heart.'

*

Marcella had taken Olivia into her confidence early on but everything she heard made her fear for Marcella in the situation.

'He's bi,' Marcella had confided.

'And are you, you know, together?'

Marcella shrugged and pouted resignedly.

'Well, yes and no.'

'So which is it?'

'It's not that binary,' Marcella said and all Olivia could think of was Venn diagrams and computer code.

'Look, the way it is, I like him more than he likes me, I know that, and in the end he'll go off with another bloke, I'm pretty sure, but why not have him while I can?'

Olivia was no good on sexual fluidity.

'I'd want to know where I stood,' Olivia said. 'People should be one thing or the other.'

'Don't be like that,' Marcella said, 'I like Jamie and trust him, how many people can you say that about?'

This was hard to argue with.

'I hope you're being careful,' Olivia said thinking of contraception.

'It's gone beyond that,' Marcella said. 'I love him regardless how it turns out. There's no shame in that.'

Despite her youth, Marcella could be quite wise.

Olivia had never had a female friend to whom she confided real secrets. She blamed her marriage break-up and a hectic life of full-time work and looking after the boys. Female friendships seemed like a leisure activity, one you'd have to devote a lot of time to and those years when the boys were small, she couldn't afford the luxury of a hobby.

When she and Marcella had one of their sessions, Olivia felt like she'd regressed to adolescence and those long mournful talks about romance that she'd never had as a teenager. She shared about Bernard.

'Tell him what you feel,' Marcella had said.

'It's not as simple as that. I don't know what I feel.'

'Well, tell him that.'

'But I want to be sure. . .'

'But you can't be. Move in close to him. As long as he's just an argument in your head, you can keep him at a distance.'

'But what if I hurt him?'

'Don't,' Marcella said.

Olivia noticed Marcella hadn't asked what if Bernard hurt her.

'It's a risk. Everything's a risk,' Marcella said. 'Being here's a risk.'

'You mean Trinity?'

'I mean life.'

*

'It was after you left,' Marcella says. Olivia feels obscurely to blame as if her leaving had skewed the status quo. 'Theo assigned us to different reading groups and suddenly the whole thing seemed to disintegrate. Jamie literally ghosted me.'

She looks around nervously, then leans forward conspiratorially.

'It wasn't the sex, it was the intimacy. Know what I mean? You have a special place and then you don't and there's no explanation. It wasn't as if he replaced me with someone else. It was just like he'd dropped off the face of the earth. As if my allotted time with him was over.'

The effect of standing there whispering to one another of intimacies in the middle of the vaccination centre makes it seem like a matter of life and death.

'I mean, if he'd explained, if he'd given me warning. If he'd even texted me and told me it was over.'

Imagine, Olivia thinks, being grateful for being brushed off by text.

'But there was nothing and I didn't have the courage to confront him. . .'

'Well, he didn't leave much of an opening, did he? Just shutting off like that. And then with COVID. . .'

'All the same, I should have confronted him. But I was afraid, afraid that he'd laugh it off, whatever was between us. As if that was the way the world worked and he'd see me as a silly romantic little girl trying to make more of it than what it was.'

'Sounds to me like he was the one who couldn't deal with what was between you.'

'But that's not the worst of it. . .' Marcella begins.

Olivia scans through the possibilities – pregnancy? venereal disease? – then realises how out of date she is.

'Marcella?' another steward three lanes away shouts at her. 'Can you come here for a minute?'

Marcella scurries off leaving Olivia dangling.

*

She thought when she printed out 'A Man In Reserve' for the workshop, it would grow, become substantial, but the content just seemed flimsier in typescript. In particular, she was dreading Jamie and Marcella's verdicts. Even though they'd known one another only two months, she felt close to them, bolstered by their opinion of her. She liked how Marcella called her Liv without even asking – it made her feel as if she'd become another person inside the gates of Trinity. She'd given no hint of what she was writing about. Jamie and Marcella talked about their writing all the time but Olivia felt that was taboo. Anyway she couldn't talk about it in the way Jamie did. How could she be articulate about her incoherence? But her worries were unfounded. That first time, the others were kind, if only by omission. Carl said her story was a bit timid. It's pretty formless, Jamie said, I mean it doesn't go anywhere, doesn't lead us to anything but more confusion. But, Marcella counter-argued, isn't that just like life? It's autofiction, drawn from life and not neatly tied up into some conclusion to satisfy the dictates of an arbitrary fictional form. As she listened to them fighting over her, Olivia felt like the child of divorcing parents.

It is not a story yet, Theo Bender said, it is a draft. She could feel the wind whistling through the thin stuff of her narrative and imagined a piece of Swiss cheese. She was grateful that Theo had been so diplomatic, but she couldn't escape the feeling the others were all soft-peddling because they didn't feel her work was worth savaging. She'd seen them fillet Carl's magic realism fables, and dismiss Dermot's painful rural coming-of-age stories as tractor fiction. It wasn't like they couldn't be forthright. Olivia felt like they were being kind to the elderly.

You must try again, Theo Bender said. And remember this. Fiction is reality transformed.

*

After Marcella disappears, Olivia shuffles up two, then three places in the queue. They are lined up in a roped gangway like at an airport check-in, their prescribed distances marked out with yellow lozenges on the floor. She can see that Marcella is in deep consultation with the other steward who holds a clipboard. Come on, Olivia thinks, hurry, or else I'll never hear the end of the story. She moves up to the top of the queue. This isn't like the checkout line; you can't volunteer someone to go ahead of you, can you?

Marcella comes hurrying back.

'So what, what did he do?' she asks. She has been racking her brains trying to think what transgression Jamie was guilty of.

'He stole my novel,' Marcella says.

Somehow Olivia was expecting something more catastrophic.

'You know the Jane Eyre novel I mentioned earlier? I gave him the first half of it to read and he decided to write his own version, though he never told me.'

So nothing to do with sexual politics in the end.

'My idea was to have Jane's spiteful cousin John Reid attempt to rape her. And that's why she's sent off to that terrible boarding school. Because nobody believes her. Like a historical #JaneEyre too story. That's as far as I'd got. I was a bit stuck so I asked him to take a look at it.'

There are bright tears in her eyes behind the enormous spectacles.

'I trusted him entirely. I just never thought. . .'

'Did he use your material?'

'Oh no, just the idea.'

Is it a crime to steal someone else's idea, Olivia wonders.

'He's turned it into a coming-of-age gay story from John Reid's point of view. He's made it first person. He's made it all about himself.'

'How do you know if you haven't been in touch?

'Oh, he told me after the fact. When he'd finished, he rang up, finally, to tell me what he'd done. That's why he broke up with me, he said. He cut me off *before* he did the dirty on me. It was a pre-emptive strike.'

'Oh Marcella, I'm so sorry.'

'And the worst of it is, he doesn't think he's done anything wrong. It's totally different to yours, he kept on saying. There's room for two John Reid novels in the world. Except that his is finished and with an agent in London.'

*

When Christmas intervened, Olivia was relieved to get away from Trinity. Six weeks at home with only the boys to worry about and one measly recalcitrant story to fix felt manageable. She could do that. Bernard was back and she'd invited him for Christmas dinner. He came armed with his pictures of China. Charlie had set up a screen in the living room and put the images on a loop so they could see them in full glorious technicolour. The boys, bless them, entered into the spirit and ooh and aahed in the right places. The images of the Forbidden City, The Great Wall, the Chinese warriors, dappled the living room in pearly light. The screen was visible through the serving hatch, weirdly miniaturised, as they ate in Olivia's kitchen. Every so often, through dinner, Bernard would halt mid-chew and say – ah this was when we went to Beijing – but although he was full of talk about the other people on the organized trip, Olivia couldn't shake the feeling that the experience had been a disappointment. She wondered if she'd set him up for that, with all her dire warnings about the hypocrisy of new age communism, the human rights abuses, the Uighir Muslims. She'd really wanted to dampen his unbridled enthusiasm; she'd wanted to shake him out of his wilful innocence as if he believed he could travel without any responsibility for the conditions at the other end. Not for the first time she examined her conscience with regard to Bernard and found herself wanting.

Remembering Marcella's advice, she chided herself all through Christmas Day - stop keeping your distance, move in. (Which sounded like writing advice to her.) Be kind (Which didn't.) But she couldn't do it. When Bernard donned his gold paper crown and danced with Mal's new girlfriend after dinner, she could feel a great chasm opening up between them and she could only see him as an unfortunate fat man who'd accidentally gate-crashed their Christmas.

You're a bitch, Olivia Fletcher, she thought, a total bitch.

*

'You'll write something else though, won't you. You won't give up?'

Marcella looks at her oddly.

'Of course,' she says hotly. 'I won't let Jamie Hickson have the satisfaction of wrecking my career.'

She leans forward, too close for comfort or safety, and hisses in Olivia's ear. 'I hope he catches COVID and dies.'

*

She'd been accused of being timid; well, no more! You have a lifetime's more experience than any other student in the room, she told herself as she redrafted 'A Man in Reserve', use it! But the deafening silence that initially greeted the second draft should have alerted her.

'First thoughts?' Theo asked.

Olivia knew enough to know they were not lost for words – when was Jamie Hickson ever stuck for words? – they were with-holding them.

'Anyone?' Theo prompted.

Olivia was reminded of the first day. She even felt tempted to step in herself and apologise for the story so great was the tension, but the rules didn't allow for that.

'It has no literary merit,' Carl said finally. 'It's sub-par romance. There's no depth, no resonance. The lovers – who aren't really lovers – are not believable and the narration just sits there stating its case.'

'You're too far away from your characters so it just becomes Mills and Boon,' monosyllabic Dermot said, 'sorry, Oliv.'

'Precisely,' Jamie chimed in. 'Janet Malcolm says the fictional character is a being with no privacy who stands before the reader naked and exposed but these people – he smacked the manuscript with his hand – these people are flat and opaque and dressed up in full battle gear.'

'I agree,' Marcella said. 'They don't let us in.'

Some of the others, whom she cared less about, offered their opinions. Then the workshop dwindled into silence.

'Why don't they just fuck one another?' Jamie said at last. He seemed exasperated at Olivia and she couldn't understand how suddenly it had become so personal.

'Exactly!' Marcella chimed in. 'I mean why won't this woman – Paulette, Jesus what a name! – put up or shut up? She's so weak and so vain. And so vacillating.'

Olivia felt the stab of betrayal. How could Marcella be so cruel when she'd confided the real live experience behind the story?

'She despises him, what's that all about?' Marcella went on.

Olivia's face was aflame. She was afraid she was going to cry – or leak from the eyes. In her sixties, even her tears were ungenerous.

'Can we not write about weak and vain characters?' Theo intervened, but it wasn't to defend Olivia, it was to take up Marcella's point. But it took the attention off her.

'We can,' Jamie answered, 'but we have to do it with conviction.'

'And without resorting to cliché,' Marcella added for good measure.

Theo Bender had the last word.

'This is writing for therapy, Olivia, but it's not reaching for Art.'

It was always said with a capital A. In Theo Bender's world that was her capital crime.

She remembered filing out of the workshop in a daze. Condemned by a jury of her peers. Jamie and Marcella asked her to come for a drink as if nothing had happened but she couldn't face it. She felt as she had the first day. Innocent and enormously foolish. She didn't belong here; she never had. It wasn't that she hadn't the brains; it was that her ambition wasn't high-brow enough. Years of dulling necessary work had knocked that out of her. Life and single mothering and bad TV had thinned her emotions. The bad poetry of her youth at least had had heart.

She stayed on for a couple of weeks but she'd already decided. Oddly, she didn't want Jamie and Marcella to feel responsible. Not for their sake, but for her own. She had her pride. She stopped going to classes in February. For a few weeks she sent in a doctor's note – burnout, he'd written – then she stopped doing even that. It was good timing; it meant there was never a day of reckoning. A month later COVID drove everything online and it gave her the perfect excuse; she couldn't have handled the technology. Or the remoteness. After all, she'd wanted a campus experience. It wasn't the boot camp ethos or even the generation gap that defeated her in the end. Nor was it low self-esteem or the lack of a sense of entitlement that seemed to dog women of her age, the second-chance crowd. As an ordinary citizen of Dublin, she'd never once set foot on Front Square. Now, she'd got used to striding around Trinity as if she owned the place. That was something, wasn't it?

But the reason she couldn't continue was Bernard.

Not only was her fiction all about Bernard, but since his return he'd been pestering her to show him what she was writing. (He offered it as a trade for suffering through his Chinese slide show.) She realised she couldn't show him anything because all she'd written about was him. Reams and reams of Bernard. She couldn't stop. Every man in her fiction was fat, self-deprecating, entirely loveable in the abstract. Her father figures, her invented husbands, were all the same. Every woman was her – sharp and prickly when anyone came near, still holding out for someone better. Or just holding out for the sake of it? Because it had become habit. There was nothing elevating in what she wrote, nothing transformative. Her plain truth was just too plain. And too revealing.

*

'Next!' a steward further up the line calls out at Marcella.

'That's you,' Marcella says.

She wants to reach out and hug Marcella but she'd probably be done for deadly assault attempting to hug a steward at a vaccination centre. Damn this bloody disease, Olivia thinks, that forces us to rely on words. She thinks of offering her phone number. But why? What comfort could she be to Marcella? She'd warned her that Jamie would break her heart and so it had come to pass. Just not in the way she'd anticipated. There was no comfort in being right.

'So long then,' she says and Marcella gives her a miniature wave, like you would to a small child.

*

If the tent outside reminded her of third world democracy, then the vaccination stalls lined up in avenues, remind her of an astrologer's booth. She'd had her fortune told once at a fun-fair. It was when the boys were small and they'd egged her on because they'd wanted to go back to the shooting range on their own. She stepped through a bead curtain into a tent bathed in a brothel red light. The fortune teller sat at a card table draped in a kilim and there was a stack of cards under her right hand. She had very long false red fingernails but apart from that she was in normal gear. Olivia was slightly disappointed at her homely look. She had jaded blonde hair, crepey skin at the neck and had flat, fleshy inexpressive face. Embarrassingly, she wore a pale lilac twinset which Olivia had also bought in M & S but had never worn because she thought it was too matronly. So in some weird way it was like looking at herself in a decade's time. Already, her future being laid out. Olivia didn't remember much about the session. There was the dealing and fingering of the playing cards but all she remembered was the woman told her she would meet the man of her dreams in a large public space. She imagined a hospital, an airport terminal, even a university campus. She'd tried them all. No luck.

*

Her vaccinator has berry brown skin and nut-coloured hair. She gives off a vibrant healthy glow. How does she manage it stuck inside a vax centre from morning till night. Wild swimming, the nurse tells her. This is what used to be called swimming in the sea before it was branded into a new activity by the pandemic (which requires a whole new set of paraphernalia – wet suits and dry robes.) She urges Olivia to try it and Olivia doesn't have the heart to tell her she can't swim. As the boys got older, she'd tried her hand at hobbies, but braving the sea was never going to be one of them. Too much immersion for her.

The nurse jabs her so expertly she's still waiting for the sting when she carefully begins rolling down Olivia's sleeve.

Afterwards, like everybody else, she's directed to the observation area where she's told she'll have to wait for 10 minutes in case of a bad reaction. The folding chairs are set two metres apart and the place looks for all the world like an examination hall without the desks. Even though it's full of old people, people the same age as her, people with the same birthdays even, Olivia is assailed by youthful memories. Discos and dances where, who knew, some of these same men and women were in attendance. For a minute she feels again the buzz of apprehension, of possibility. How ridiculous, she chastises herself. We're in the middle of a pandemic and you're thinking about youthful sex. Cop yourself on, she tells herself, but she can't shift the resurrected feelings. What has prompted it, she wonders. Seeing Marcella again? Or is it the atmosphere of shuffling uncertainty in the hall, now caused by stiffening limbs, then by emotional ineptitude. She looks at some of these solid, white-haired men and can see the younger men they were. The women come in the same types they did 40 years ago – there are the trim flirtatious ones in crisp casuals, except now they have ash-coloured hair or have gone blonde, and the dowdy heavier ones who've left themselves go and are wearing runners for their fallen arches. Even the ones leaning on sticks don't look that old to her, but that's a delusion, she knows that.

The local radio station is piped through the speakers in the observation area *Saturday Night Fever* comes on. Suddenly in the midst of all this patient, biddable old age, she wants to get up and dance. She wants to see all these old men and women up on their bunioned feet with their untamed locks and their tired leisure wear. She wants to see them revert to the lazy sashaying they called dancing in the 70s. That won't be a stretch, will it? She imagines them, the walking wounded, joining a conga line and shunting and swaying around the vax centre gathering up strays as they go. They'll work up a sweat and it'll be a good thing, not a cause for alarm. The vaccinators and stewards will join in, applauding their plucky, joyful elders. Her feet start to tap and she thinks to hell with it, I'm going to do it anyway, and she rises shimmying her hips and fisting the air. It's like the dole scene in *The Full Monty* except no one joins her.

She sees a steward – not Marcella – stalking towards her and she sits down abruptly, just at the point where she can see the others were contemplating getting up. Oh well, too late. Then it strikes her. If Bernard were here, he'd join her; he's a terrific dancer, always has been.

She picks up her phone.

'Are you free?' she texts, all fingers and thumbs.

Two Poems
John Goodby

Im wunderschönen Monat Mai

In the drop-dead gorgeous May
when tree-buds were burgeoning
in Brynmill's Latin Quarter
I ran my true feelings up a flagpole
to see if anyone would salute them.

In the drop-dead gorgeous May
birds chirruping & the physical
side of it quite quite over I was free
to tell her & no strings I actually
harboured these, like, tender thoughts.

Und wüßten's die Blumen, die kleinen

If the little flowers just knew
how cut up I can get
they'd weep out of solidarity
to well   ease my pain

& if the nightingales were only aware
how sad & sickly I am
they'd kick up a fantastic racket
their revivifying warble

& if they had an inkling of my woes
the tiny golden stars
they'd clamber down from their spheres
& whisper comfort unto me

& out past Mumbles pier the moon
sheds her benignant glow on Sin
City & Wind Street's Friday ruck
& would help out if she divined my ache

but none of them can really know it
there's just one who gets my *schmerz*
the exact same one who diced
in tiny pieces this old fool heart

Three Poems
Taz Rahman

Missa Solemnis

*(Scene: A plaque for Dr Christopher Hoddell, 1957-94, on a Llandaff
Cathedral cemetery bench)*

Rust mildew
     shapes in rain
     two feet shy, leaves

 glyph runes
     on oily ravines
     wet skin

macerate
     stories gone
     fables to tell

a nook of leaves.
     Tonight, cyclops
     may gobble satyrs

the dark is finding shape
     wagtails may rouge cheeks
     line boundaries

define moments, let the gone
     gawk at faces
     edging a sinking sun.

In a step (or two)
        the last light arcs in
        vespers curling

stone cracks, the dark
        clamps ancient rock, moss
        hems the fog

in the field behind
        probing, *is it time*
        to head back

        or *a time to start?*

The caterpillar cleans
        itself each summer
        at the end of each

unpredictable stint of
        rain, a stout beak
        yellows the skin

in the fading light, is it
        a shag or a cormorant
        tickling Taff?

How to tell
        the difference, what
        defray, promises

made to lips
        sat on a bench, backs
        pressed in anticipation

pressing a rectangle
    a small golden plaque
    Kyrie, Credo, Agnus Dei.

A Pond for All Eels

How vibernum clatters primrose
    the heron greys spring
        hangs like a lamp giving off gloom

how the twigs lurch at each crotch
    as bodies float on the wings
        of their macs

how eels electric
    transcutaneously, motor
        neurons

how sparrows embroider decisions
    in brown not saying a word
        braille bushes

I want to make room for the body
    for its speechless want to be
        clattered

I want to pretend that
    a day was a night, blame
        the breeze

some eels emit a weak pulse
    to navigate, find prey, melt icebergs
        linger in a set of eyes

I want to be a stream
    discover the shallows
        where duckweed congeals

green and dark eyes
    bloat spring, hum bells
        kill time.

Turning Saints into the Sea

Stubborn pink scales a cliff-face becoming heather,
the sea crests hours instructing gulls to remember
nothing, footsteps totter in throat knots like a past

actuating days deigning the corners of each thirst,
meaningful as the sum of parts. Foxgloves stare
at distant elders wanting to grow tall, clumps of clay

grieve particle separation in tattered pots, spoon
voices pretending that words whispered here could
be heard in the furthest west of land where the fit

for communion jam a deceased willow, bodies
aureate song shaping ampersands. Dead-wood
feels no urge to chase the day after, a rotting boat

bobs twice a day for brief spells to sky-gaze inches
higher contemplating what penetrates its shell peeling
a shore to illicit touch, an axis fit for a crushed pigeon

who sacrificed himself in flight to remember a June
ending under a city ash for flesh to go their own way.

Everything Falling
Emily Devane

Cambridge unsteadied Helena: took the air from her lungs; squeezed her so hard around the chest that breathing became an effort; weakened her until she was somehow *lesser*. Just the sight of its carefully-trimmed lawns made her feeble. And when circumstances forced her to walk its traffic-darkened streets, she kept to the shadows, away from the watchful glare of dead scholars. Their eyes, now trapped in stone, retained an arrogance that never dulled. The biting wind carried their whispers as she went by: *Go back, go back: you don't belong.*

When Helena first met the third year with the ludicrous tie, she'd only just unpacked her things. A poster of Johnny Depp sucking on a cigarette, a mobile made from semi-circles of glass, painted like rainbows to catch the light. Pieces she'd lug from room to room before boxing them up in the loft. The college library smelled of clammy handshakes and books, forgotten and dusty in their jackets.

'You have a beautiful name,' he said, looking at her left breast.

She'd forgotten the badge, applied upon arrival at the drinks reception. Helena was among that year's batch of Freshers. Her gown was starch-stiff, while his was ragged with wear. And his tie, she felt, with its stripes of lime green and brown, was deliberately unappealing.

'Shakespeare's the master of unrequited love, don't you think? I always felt for Helena.' His eyes fixed greyly upon hers. 'Sherry?' He poured a glass without waiting for her reply.

The newly beautiful rarely believe it and Helena, according to the neighbour, had *turned out well, considering*. Considering what? Helena wondered, though in truth, she knew: *Considering that mother of yours.*

The neighbour was right. She'd been an unremarkable child: hair blighted by a series of attacks by her mother's scissors, a figure that could best be described as sturdy. But when dinner times came and went, her mother having forgotten all about them, Helena's curves slipped away without comment. Her hair now swung in waves down her back, her mother having forgotten about the scissors, too. Now, they had been put away for safe-keeping. Quite without meaning to – and due, in part, to neglect – she'd acquired some sort of appeal which, after a lifetime of invisibility, was not entirely welcome. It was if she'd inhabited a foreign self and was stumbling over the language.

'It means light,' she said, unravelled by his lopsided grin. 'My name, that is. But not the sunny kind,' she added. 'I was born under a full moon, whatever that means.'

'It's perfect,' he said. Then he raised his chin and let out a full-throated howl.

She put her finger to her lips, hoping to shush him, but he howled again, this time even louder than the first. Heads swivelled in their gowns. The sherry stung her throat.

The next day, he knocked on her door to return the silver scarf she'd left at the drinks reception. *A sliver of moonlight. I knew it must be yours,* he told her.

His pursuit – she likened it to a campaign of pillage – lasted a term. He began by borrowing her vinyl, returning her records with messages scratched in the parts without grooves.

'May I borrow this?' he'd say, holding the LP with reverential fingers. 'Just for the night?'

The borrowing, she suspected, was his way of insinuating himself into her world.

'Did you write this?' she once asked him. 'This word on my record?' The letters were scratched deep.

He made a point of putting on his glasses, of shaking his head.

'I know you did,' she said.

Though he denied it, a smile played at one corner of his mouth. A smile she couldn't help but notice.

'The spelling's wrong, anyway. Moonlight has a 'g' in it,' she said, with more spite than she'd intended.

At that, his shoulders fell and his face became gloomy.

How strange, she thought, how quickly he could change. She could imagine him like that, boyish. Perhaps it was his boyishness that appealed, because few people considered him handsome. He walked with more of a shuffle than a stride, hands in pockets, chin buried in his scarf, leaning forwards as if into a perpetual wind. Alone at night, when she tried to picture his face, she had trouble with his eyes. Everything about his outer self was drained of colour, from the way he dressed in faded corduroy – the ludicrous tie had been a curious exception – to his hair and eyes, which were no discernible colour at all. That day, his eyes were a bruise, heavy with accusation. She should have left it there, seen them for the warning that they were. Instead, she kissed him.

By late autumn, with the leaves rustling about their ankles, they walked arm in arm, Helena's former boyfriend dispatched by post. She had always loved autumn, the anarchy of it. Everything falling, the world transformed. That Autumn in Cambridge was spectacular.

One time, before the kiss, he came to her door. She lay starfish-like on her bed, face puffy from crying, surrounded by pages of notes. The bedspread was a patchwork quilt made from scraps of childhood dresses and pillowcases and trousers whose knees had worn through. It smelled of home. She liked to touch the material.

'What's all this?' he said.

'The tears? Or the mess?' she said, half-laughing, between sobs.

'Both,' he said, sitting beside her.

She blew her nose. 'I'm a mess too.'

'A lovely mess,' he said, and he reached over, smoothed her hair from her cheek and – in a gesture so intimate it made her redden –

licked the salt from her skin. 'Come out and play,' he said. 'We need air.'

Funny how he said *we*, as if their needs were the same.

'I'm supposed to hand this in,' she said, holding up a sheet of paper with one line of neatly looping letters. One line was all she'd written: *I can't help but feel this is a mistake.*

He tilted his head to read her words and his voice, when it came out, was oddly strained. 'You mean me?'

'You? No, of course not. You've been so *kind*.' She looked up at him, saw him flinch at her choice of words. She'd told him about her boyfriend from home. 'I mean this place. Here. *These*.' She motioned to the notes. The pages and pages of notes that she'd made, in the hope that something would make sense. Her hand rested on a patch of cream material with brown sprigs and she said: 'This was once my mother's apron.'

Without a word, he gathered the notes into a pile and crossed the room to the open window. Then, before she could make a sound, he pushed them through and let them fall.

The papers flew and swirled. One sheet wrapped itself around a lamppost, before dropping, then swooping up towards the clock tower. She had so much to say about that - but didn't.

'Let's go,' he said. He stretched out his hand and she took it.

He was making a film. This impressed her. One time, during a break in rehearsals, they met in a coffee shop where the cakes were piled high. The walls were covered with pictures of laughing clowns. A group of her friends came in and joined them for a while but he stared into his cup, barely talking.

'Have you noticed,' he said once they'd left, 'Have you noticed how everyone here does everything as a pack, like dogs?'

'I suppose.' She tugged at the lycra she wore. Someone had persuaded her to try rowing and she hadn't thought much about it. The river, the peace of it, allowed her mind to escape. 'You didn't need to make it so obvious,' she said. And she told him something she'd known for a long time: that people are drawn to each other, into groups, for no other reason than habit. That those can sometimes be the loneliest of places. She almost told him things she'd never told anyone, about her mother. But just as she opened her mouth, he began to talk.

'I've come to realise,' he said, his gaze returning to his empty cup. 'I've come to realise that our conversations are not like conversations at all. We're just two people talking at each other, without really listening.' He put a five pound note on the table and stood up as if performing a part.

Unsure what to do, she grasped his hand and drew it near. He was wearing gloves.

'Oh Helena,' he said, pulling his hand free, 'go and take a bath, or something.' A bell make a tinkling sound as he closed the door.

On the wall, the clown pictures rattled.

It was soon after that, she stopped rowing.

At home, when her mother was having one of her bad days, Helena had gone to the hills. In Cambridge, there were no hills. Well, nothing like the ones she'd run across muddied and reckless as a child. The gardens here were pristine, with little signs on the lawns urging: 'No trespassers'. Even the ducks seemed neat, as if they had been manufactured and placed along the river banks for effect. She imagined pushing them in, one by one, watching them float away. She bought a packet of cigarettes and walked along the tow-path beside the Cam. The quiet was occasionally interrupted by the rhythmic sound of a rowing eight slicing its way through the water, the rowers pink-limbed with exertion. Helena felt sickly by comparison. On a bench set back from the path, she sat, opened the cigarettes and smoked them all, from start to finish. She wasn't a smoker, not really. She wanted to feel the dirt in her lungs.

A layer of snow covered everything. He'd apologised. Was it dishonest of her not to ask why he'd been so cruel? She supposed it was. If so, she was as much to blame. She always thought that, always said that to herself.

'Isn't it lovely?' she said instead, as they stopped on a bridge that spanned the inky Cam like a piece of confection. Out here, away from the watchful courtyards, at least she could breathe. She looked at him, willed him to respond.

'You never get angry,' he said. 'It's just occurred to me that you never even raise your voice.' He looked into the water, spoke to her reflection. Snowflakes rested on his hat. His bulky coat broadened his shoulders.

'I do,' she said. 'I do. I'm just not very good at showing it. There are things I find hard. Harder than you'd imagine.'

'You're cold,' he said. 'Are you cold?'

'Not really.'

'I'll take that as a yes.' He wrapped his scarf around her neck and pulled her to him. He smelled of clean things, of soap and of order. 'My favourite place isn't far from here,' he said. 'There's something I want you to see. I know you'll love it.'

The garden at Emmanuel was a winter-perfect scene. The trees laced with white and the college windows glowing, thin curtains obscuring the silhouettes of the inhabitants beyond.

'It's magical,' she said, 'all the windows, lit up like that. Like a snow globe, or something.'

He didn't reply.

She imagined hot chocolate, a cup, warm in her hands.

'Almost there', he said, pulling her along. Their feet shuffled softly in the snow. 'I can't wait for you to see it.'

And then there it was: a huge, twisted piece of bronze rising up from the powder-white lawn.

'Walk around it,' he said.

She did as instructed, suddenly fearful of the expectant look in his eyes. The bronze was elegant, womanly – all broad hips and narrow waist and flared ribcage. Her feet made a chain of compacted prints around it.

'Do you see it?' he said, when she returned to him.

She couldn't help but feel he'd been here before, with someone else; that this was some sort of test.

'Is it a *she*?' Helena ventured.

He gave her more guesses.

'A musical note, a bird, an angel's wings?'

No, no and no again.

At last, sensing his impatience, she gave up.

'It's a smile,' he said. 'Can you not see that, Helena? A smile.' He wasn't smiling, though.

Standing there, snow falling around them, she had the absurd impression that they were trapped. Figurines in this giant snow globe, being watched, laughed at.

That night she got the call from home. Things had got worse.

Once the snow had thawed, he invited her to see the film he'd made. After, he asked: had she liked it? Of course she had, shot through as it was with the music he'd pilfered, the records he'd marked. But fearing that she'd lost him already, she gave a non-committal shrug that she knew would hurt. *Why?* He asked, over and over. *Why didn't you like it?* She shook her head, words having left her. So, that's what had become of her records: they had become a soundtrack. The dialogue was so clever, so witty. But she couldn't tell him, not now. He was right. Their conversations weren't conversations at all. They were just lines from a script. Lines he'd been trying out. Lines she hadn't known.

The end came quickly. He called her by the wrong name, then smiled at the mistake, that same knowing smile. This time, it scratched something deep inside of her. A permanent scar that collected with the others and sat beneath her ribs. The letters he sent afterwards did nothing to erase what he'd done. The new muse was pretty, in that malnourished way.

Helena took photographs that term with a camera she'd been given as a birthday present, the last one before her mother had become ill. Beautiful photographs, she liked to imagine, of trees uncloaked, silvery frozen ponds and that lopsided grin of his, close up. Perhaps a glimpse of those eyes. It wouldn't have mattered about the colour because the film was black and white. Only later, when she came to have the film developed, the man in the chemist's shook his head. Light must have got in, he said. There was nothing there. No twisted bronze, no inky Cam. Nothing. It was as if none of it had happened.

*

Twenty years on, and in London, a city whose ghosts were drowned out by noise. Helena was bolder here, put at ease by the whirring drone of the ice-cream van, the tinny thrum of headphones in other people's ears, the nearby clank of scaffolding. The paddling pool in the park had just re-opened and the day was warm, just shy of sticky.

Helena was pushing her child on a swing when she saw him, now bearded and hollow cheeked. Crouched by the sandpit, his small blonde accomplice upended a bucket to rapturous applause. They shared the same lopsided grin.

'Hi,' Helena said, a little too brightly.

The blonde child lay claim to her father's leg. 'Hi.' With a flicker of recognition, his eyes rested greyly upon hers. 'Remind me,' he said. 'Remind me of your name?'

Letter to My First Milk Tooth
Breda Spaight

Dear Lower Central Incisor, today, when I ponder
where I find the strength to continue, I think of
my first 3 years – I was primed by pain. Only months
in the world, I bawl, kick, squirm while you bud, cut
through pink gum, erupt past mucous membrane that knows
only the sweet flesh of nipple and spurts of body-warmed milk.
You, my first milk tooth, one of twenty, each a journey into
ten pairs of pain that groom me for life.
More cerebral than physical, that original pain – I am alone.
Thanks for the insight: my mother's failure, her coos,
cuddles, and carrot. I also remember your Twin,
my gratitude for their scorpion sting of loss.

By the way, when you meet your cousins
Upper Central Incisor & Twin say I said, *Nice one.*
How I yearned for my job in the Institute,
but in truth yearned to associate
with the well-dressed, the well-read, people
for whom film was not popcorn and Tom Cruise.
The disappointment. And the disappointment
in myself was a bomb blast, a mirror
with my face in a city of rubble.

Just now, I remember Elena – a starship that beams me up
from my father's house into laughter. Alcoholic, voyeur,
words I articulate like a foreigner, which bloom with Elena.
                    A shotgun guns her
into a marriage of bruise, cheater, and towards the choice

to ghost her friends. Her decision is a well where my trust sinks
and doubt springs. I'm uncertain what I want to convey
to Upper Lateral Incisor & Twin. Say I wrote.
Say I mentioned them.

When joy strikes, it drops me into a skydive freefall:
my promotion at the Institute a jolt, me – a night school
scrimping waitress. The panorama, the earth large
and small at once, cute as a toy farm. From afar, people
are kind, generous, beautiful because I – belonging –
am kind, generous, beautiful.
                              Canine Lower & Twin know
the outcome: the parachute grounded, flat as a flayed skin.

Let me tell you about Scruff – a Jack Russell, 7, a tumour,
euthanized in the back garden. April. When the drug flows
his much-tickled tummy flattens, his white chest caves,
his oomph unchained from this life of enduring the stronger.
At 64, the dead body of a spirit I love is warm on my lap.
I hadn't grieved for my mother, at 14. Her bones are bare
and memory of her is turf smoke when I do. I want to cry
in real time as Scruff's body cools, to sense his heart marvel:
rest at last. Cherry blossoms, a swallow, his nose. So young
– my mother.
I send my warmest regards to Canine Upper & Twin.

A card arrived in June. Dear Breda, We're proud of you.
We worried when Claire gained tenure ahead of you
at the Institute. Envy is hard.
          Best wishes,
               Lower Lateral Incisor & Twin.
I chose a card with a butterfly to reply. ... *and the shame*
when the blue coat with black velvet cuffs sat
near my green gabardine at mass. I said,
it's not the coat I envy, I envy breakfast

I don't make myself, breakfast
that isn't only tea and bread, breakfast table
cleared when I arrive in from school; a break
from the tightrope of my mother's moods. Envy, I said,
pivots on the pluck to survive.

Just now in the kitchen, the man who loves me rattles mugs.
He will say my name soon. There must be something wrong
with me, or wrong with love. At times, I question if it exists.
I never longed for this boy as I had for others. He was sudden
as a glare you shield your heart from. I almost shatter
it all from fear that anything golden can last.
Once, he tells me I'm a jumble of broken china. The image
is clear – blue and white chunks, some with willow, another
with fronds, a triangle with traces of the bridge – the pattern
perfect in its brokenness: dread and love in a tug-of-war. The prize –
I keep emerging from my chaos, bolder, the pieces whole: a posy
of bluebells and snowdrops.
On that note, please, give my love
to First Molar Upper & Lower, & Twins.

Finally, I enclose 'The Journey' by Mary Oliver. Just between us,
I wallow in guilt until her narrow pillar of lines save me.
I'm the poem's protagonist – *you* – ragged girl with one chance
to scatter from *your* father's house, with no choice
but to desert *your* young brother. His name
white silence on half the page – the quiet I
shrug off like the snow of sorrow I huddle under.
Please, give the poem to Second Molar Upper
& Lower, & Twins. Tell them I honour their hours of push,
push, like labour. Like labour, forgotten: my bloody
vernixed life in my own hands.

Success is counted sweetest...
Fiona O'Connor

Looked at that way it was a point she'd reached, and the picture suggested landscape although it was the figure, or figures, seemingly its subject.

Androgynous nude in an African mask looking out at the viewer; upper arm banded like a warrior, pencil-drawn. You noticed then a small mask-like face within a further blank head, floating on the surface. And just behind, indiscernible until you'd stared hard at the piece for a time, another faintly drawn presence: primitive bull head and body sequestered in a timeless place.

That's how she saw it.

Her drawing on a gallery wall. Not really - her new friend Isabella's living room in Brixton turned pop-up gallery for the weekend. Everything hung in a mixture of excitement and feared failure: nobody truly believed. Nobody could quell a sense of the ridiculous waiting for them. Too many missed moments since they first left art school, ambitions still cosseted in that swaddling of college make-believe, but not long before it all began to seem embarrassing, facing the reality of the marketplace.

She and her sister Detta, art all their childhoods. Twin sisters, Detta and Phyllis, not identical, though close enough to stand out in the clamour of styled self-image the students created.

Her own look she had maintained a decade on. A downplay of Levis and shirts, a bit Patti Smith - seventies t-shirts or fifties Mexican blouses, always something interesting in the signalling for those who could read. By contrast, Detta had worn full-on dresses in primary colours and jangly bracelets. Her sister then: round-hipped and breasted, whereas now she was as thin as a rake.

He-ey girlfriend! Isabella in silver platform boots came clunking down the stairs beaming.

Looks better on this wall don't you think? Isabella had spent the last two days arranging and rearranging the work.

Mmmn.

Did she really think so? What she felt was an unsettling exposure: her work, produced when the children were in bed or doing stuff that didn't require her, declaring itself as art.

Rare occurrences these days, her careful small drawings. Suggestive of mythological place, or so she hoped; nowhere-land inhabited by strange figures. And never a face.

The method hit on the winter their money ran out and then the paint, she and her partner J.J. - sculptor and now a trainee art teacher.

After the first baby was born they put everything they could scrape up into buying a one-bedroomed flat over a bookie's on Shooter's Hill. The baby slept with them in the huge bed Detta had bequeathed them, just before she and Peter left London for good.

With the baby breastfed and sleeping in her lap Phyllis could draw. The sketching took her off to a sense of familiar estrangement, as in her dreams.

She didn't miss colour although that had been her thing; swathes of colour in short blunt brushstrokes, building up in layers to a point of extreme energy within the canvas. When it had worked; often it eluded her, turning into a dog's dinner, meaningless, dead.

The winter of no colour had been a point of no return.

She had let her hair resort to its beginnings of grey as well. Enough with the henna from the health food shop, hours with a plastic bag around her head while the mud dried.

J.J.'s hair was dark and curly, already greying at the temples. Now they began to look the same, as some couples grow to do over the years.

She drew seriously at first, stealing time, forming the hours for it out of letting everything else go; the flat was a mess, and she loved order, normally.

Like the pencils she went through, her sense of herself was whittled down to these hours of her infant's capricious sleep. Heavy in the crook of her left arm her little one, as her right side moved and stroked, glided, shifted, her hand feeling the texture of good paper beneath it, fingers the planed wood of a pencil or ashen of charcoal.

Pleasure was in the quiet sounds made; a pattern of scratching, rubbing, marks eddying and flowing and the baby breathing, as she breathed. She'd be away, distanced from herself and the trick was to avoid making sense of the lines, the shading as it progressed. Delay its becoming until the whole looked back at her as a question, one she couldn't begin to answer.

How she'd understood it then: a humble drawing, small scale - five inches by nine – posing the unanswerable, the effing ineffable.

They laughed, she and J.J., at the poverty of her rhetoric; it seemed a just response to the grandiosity, as they had begun to speak of it, of her sister's husband's work.

Peter, the 'brother in law' – that term still distasteful to Phyllis – was suddenly, seemingly without effort on his part, huge in the art world.

He'd never been much liked.

Detta, rather, who the students had judged to be the real thing. Detta who had astounded everyone by flunking out in the last semester before graduation. Not even bothering to show her work; a gesture perceived as magnificent self-sabotage, almost more impressive than the work ever could be.

Especially given how assiduously they'd all put themselves up for grading. Even the most radical among them were working through nights to reach some imagined apogee of success, represented by a red dot on a frame.

His work by contrast, Peter's, had never been rated by the students. *Overstated understatement,* someone had drawled. *Architects' illustration* somebody else said, and that became the received pronouncement.

They were giant canvases painted in oil or mixed media: blue-grey 70s office blocks and ochre cityscapes, urban tunnels beneath overpasses, flat fields in sparrow-brown but for the pale blur of a concrete bunker or a single, distant figure: so anodyne as to produce scorn in the irony-steeped, neo-conceptual class in the noughties.

Detta had turned up to the graduation private viewing. She wore a long turquoise fairly low cut satin dress and a wreath of tiny purple-black violets in her black hair.

She had stood close to Peter throughout the opening; they held hands even as Peter's tutor introduced him to the notorious White Cube curator.

Conspicuous to every student was the length of time this guy spent on Peter's portion of the show, leaving soon afterwards without even glancing at other work.

Only later, when the event was winding down, did Detta detach herself from Peter to look for her sister.

In a corner of the hanger-sized space Phyllis' work was struggling for attention. She was stuck between enormous draped in black polyurethane forms and a deluge of blood-scrawled paper columns coiling down from the ceiling. A looped recording of heavy industry erupted every few minutes.

Hi. Phyllis said it coldly and looked away letting her sister know how much she disapproved of her choices lately. And not only that, but of the fact that Detta had left her out, completely, from her thinking, her decisions, her life, actually. The first time in *their* lives such a thing had happened.

Detta stood before her sister's best work. The one, the only one, Phyllis was happy with. She observed Detta in profile: familiar features, her own almost but not; her own perfected in her sister's.

This one's good.

The long neck from the swept up hair and slope of her shoulders, the swell of her bosom, her tanned arms against that lively blue-green and her clever hands fiddling with the satin, until Phyllis noticed a plain gold band.

What's that? She pointed to the ring.

We got married. This morning – hence the dress, and the flowers, Detta shrugged.

They were silenced. The recording switched on; noise obliterated the space for anything other than single-minded endurance.

Detta winced then laughed, winced then laughed. She put her ringed hand to her womb and so everything was understood.

*

Christ no! J.J. muttering to his phone, his head down but his eyes finding Phyllis across Isabella's crowded living room.

He was on duty with the kids, letting her have some time. Isabella was just then pointing out to her someone in the crowd she should meet, so she didn't really notice. Actually, Phyllis was avoiding noticing them; with the kids straining to get out of this adult hellhole, the slightest acknowledgment from her would bring down every negotiated constraint.

That guy just got two works into Victoria Miro's. And his work's a load of balls.

Yeah, but he's got a cock so…cock an' balls, I rest my case.

It was Phyllis' role: feeder to Isabella's rages.

Hey Bella, great space. What you've done here.

Jimmy - the Japanese – why he was called that nobody knew - in a yellow polyester suit; behind him his boyfriend, kimono-ed in blue; a teenager with hip-length light brown hair.

Hello lovelies.

Kissing and sparkling: court rituals rippled through the room. Sharp eyes though, and brittle laughter. Frequent raps on the front door, everyone noticing as more bodies slipped in, exclamations adding to the rising din.

No-one seemed much interested in the work - they looked for what they expected to find, and there it was. The real interest was in the body of the crowd. Soon the party turned away from the surrounding display, turned inwards, inevitably.

Fucksake Celia, how can you stand up in those *shoes*.

Hey!

This one's just got a residency in Norwich.

Get out. Oh *my* God!

Following Isabella into the kitchen, Phyllis left her safe zone opposite her drawing in its thin copper frame, included in the price, though she'd no expectation of a sale; it wasn't that kind of show; they were all artists - every kind of work stuffed away everywhere.

What to do with product when the product was your essential self?

Her solution had been to minimise. Like Emily Dickinson, J.J. said once, when she was wretched.   Sometimes J.J. could save her from herself. Emily's pencilled fasicles; notations on the innards of used envelopes, uselessness transformed. She'd loved that.

Isabella, fuck, fabulous, really well *done*, Bella.

Mama?

Her eldest had broken through J.J.'s cordon.

Yes.

I'm hungry.

There's food, look. On the table.

McDonald's, ple-ease.

No way.

Her child rummaged her hand into her mother's jeans' pocket - the small hand, darker-hued than her own, like a little rodent finding the warmth of her with familiar fingers.

Stop.

She extracted the pearl-tipped hand and held it in her own.

Come upstairs, Isabella commanded with a conspiratorial tone and started up herself, following Jimmy and the boy with the long hair.

Listen, tell daddy I said he could take the two of you to McDonald's. And when you get back we'll go home, ok?

Her girl disappeared into the crowd.

*

After the graduation, the students sitting on the bed passing lines to each other. It was pastiche, not the thing itself. She wasn't stoned: some kind of proxy state, manufactured more than altered; they were on an assembly line to pleasure, jammed together on the sagging bed, the students, now new graduates.

And where was the new bride?

Hendrix - on CD – toujours pastiche. They acted out amongst the rubble of times not their own.

They had always played. Galactic imaginings even in solitude as kids. With mud and grass, feathers and sticks, anything fluid or sticky that could be worked through, rubbed away, smeared.

They looked in on alien forms, she and her sister. Hidden in burrowed holes beneath hedges, they watched. How uncanny a normal day was; those empty interludes when nothing moved; rows of houses, concrete and glass, standing, waiting.

She and her sister, whispers in code, heads turning towards the same micro-spectacle at the same instant: raindrops edging an iron gate, quiver of breeze, they fall together.

Where was she?

*

We're up here, Isabella called to her from the second landing.

Her new best friend Bella, orbits pulled together by their children's lives. At the school gates, although neutralised as parents like all the others, yet they stood out for each other. They recognised affinities in their struggle to work, to hold on when the possibilities for their art grew smaller.

It wasn't that important.

What wasn't? She closed the door softly behind her as Isabella signalled.

That thing they said in the film about Peter. Growing up on a council estate, all that.

Here. Jimmy offered up the mirror striped in white lines.

Thanks.

Rubbish documentary, Jimmy said.

Great-white-male cliché, his lover said, dragging his fingers back through his hair in a fluid gesture.

Terrible. Isabella topped up her glass.

Thanks.

Looked gorgeous though, the light and everything. The sea, Jimmy said.

God yeah. Isabella lay back against the pillowed headboard. That beautiful house. I mean, why can't people just be happy? Get on with it. You're in Paradise fucksake.

Phyllis wouldn't take the bait. She was rolling up a ten pound note, very concentrated. She knew they were waiting for her to take them there. Paths through tropical gardens, breakfasts looking out onto tree-tops, oranges pulled from boughs on the sparkling veranda. More: steep white steps up the side of the house to Peter's studio. His paintings, dozens of them lying about, worth so much. How was it possible?

She put the rolled tenner to her nostril with a hiding gesture. As though picking your nose, she always thought. She snorted quickly. Yeah, it's really something.

Detta in the vast marble and steel kitchen with its view of the bay, listening out for the children, for him. Keeping it exactly as he needed. And her sobbing the night before she was leaving to come home. Letting Phyllis in then, finally, when she had to go.

She passed the mirror back, saw how the boy was watching her - the look of appraisal was familiar - proximity to greatness? Her?

Stunning, Isabella said. And so, so sad, the break-up, with the kids and stuff.

Everything is fucking sad when you think about it, long-haired boy said. Don't get me wrong, he said.

*

The students on the bed doing rubbish coke; this was their defining moment - she could see it now. The winning ticket had already been drawn and nothing they could do about that.

Detta, where was she?

A hole in the room where her sister should have been, and Peter. But they had decided between themselves to grow up. They were gone; they wouldn't be back for her.

The sagging bed was a ship of fools. They yelled, rolled on the heaving decks. Someone took his clothes off, they whooped and howled. Someone threw her shoes at the ceiling light. Someone stood up shouting Fuck Blair, and Fuck Brown, and Fuck Damien fucking arsehole fucking Hirst. They roared. It was the saddest day of her life and she was laughing hard until J.J. asked, what's up? And then she was crying, sitting on the floor.

The ship of fools draped a duvet over her and J.J., so that became a thing – the couple tending to each other's wounds, lifeboat couple drifting off, not meant to be but how it turned out.

Peter's rise was their fall, the whole lot of them, class of 99, but especially hers, as she was the twin not chosen.

*

Lines from a pencil point, you followed them; they did not follow you; when it was working.

At college she'd been obsessed with pencil strengths – softest as strongest. And paper of course, the receiving ground, terrain for her wandering.

Shading the underneath of a breast, her hand cradling the lead between fingers and thumb, expressing a rhythm freed of her control.

She would remember this, black shade gathering, finding form, her heart beating in elation, and trepidation that it might stop.

Everything was held on a thread in the overheated old studio; bus rattles outside, misery light through the roof windows spattered by dirty rain; the students and their easels semi-circling their model whose heavy flesh was a tumble into shadows, curvatures emerging like moons out of night.

To her left, Peter, not doing much it seemed, his arms folded, just watching. As aware, she sensed, of her work, as she was of his. A step to the paper then to make his mark, back again to observing.

He was gathered into her own motion. They were together in this thing, this veneration. His work, her work; feeding each other with the power of their attention; his breaths, hers; this recognition: theirs. Or so she'd imagined.

The students couldn't but she'd seen it. What he *didn't* do that singled him out. Even the tutors failed to recognise it, most of them.

Better to fail better than succeed like that, she'd said to him of a mediocre tutor's work, after reading Beckett. She'd given him her copy of Molloy, and then Malone Dies. Whatever she gave him he read because he hadn't read anything. Consumed was what he was. Everything was open for exploration. That was his genius and Phyllis saw it.

Her sister had disagreed; she thought his work showed a mean streak. She said it was devoid of something. Of what? Phyllis had demanded. Detta just shrugged, said she didn't know. But maybe it was what had lured her away from her own talent.

Give this chick another line before her brats turn up, Isabella ordered.

Here you go, Jimmy held out the poisoned chalice.

Detta had sent over her baby's clothes in boxes stamped Port of Spain. As Phyllis' daughter grew she sent them back because Detta was pregnant again. And then the same boxes arrived once more for her own second child, when Peter's first big show at MOMA was going up and Detta wrote that she would need them yet again in a few months.

It was kind of a joke; certainly by that stage Detta didn't need second-hand baby clothes - at Sotheby's Peter's painting, Cabin on the Lake, reached the highest price ever paid for a work by a living artist.

In different ways the parcels had become a register of their own work in progress: Detta embroidering on some of the tiny vests and wraps, the soft nightcaps: bluebirds and palm trees and flying boats, even on the miniscule socks. Then Phyllis trying out her own embellishments; giant snails driving red buses, skipping sausages chased by policemen in Bobby hats; stories being told in images across little chest-widths and bum curves. Like veins trailing across the sea, she felt, the threads in and out of the baby clothes were pulling their sisterhood closer.

For his thirtieth she sent Peter a copy of Dickinson's collected poems. She wanted him to know of Emily in her long white dress. Really though, she wanted him to remember *her*, the twin who might have been the one.

He didn't acknowledge. He was very busy, they were filming a documentary about his work, Detta said.

*

She was more stoned than she wanted to be by the time her kids came back, smelling of chips, darting eyes signalling the sugar rush.

Isabella demanded a dance with J.J. The kids were racing around. Jimmy's boy with the long hair sat curled on a sofa watching them. Like a cat taking notes, was her thought, and she realised she'd internalised a conversation with her far-away sister, newly divorced, something she hoped might bring them closer still.

The scarred cavity of Detta's removed breast was a shocking image she carried.

You look flummoxed, her sister had said.

They'd been swimming in the turquoise glass of the Caribbean. Peter wasn't there.

He's with his girlfriend, Detta said. He still uses the studio. This is where he paints. She said it with defiance, as though testifying to the camera.

It was the last day of her visit to her sister. They'd gone down to the beach for a final swim. Later they got a bit drunk. The children had fallen asleep early, tired out by the excitement and the climb back up to the house.

Black ink was the medium. They were lulled into whispering by the breathing of the waves below.

Two faces she held in her memory of that night, although she had only seen one, glowing in candlelight: her sister's, her own.

The house was high on a cliff jutting from the forest, hoisted up, audacious.

The greater Peter's success, the higher we had to climb, Detta said. She wafted her hand at the surrounding house. Her tears then, out of nowhere, exposing the distance between them - Phyllis had known nothing of all this.

I could stay on you know? Help with the kids. She thought first of Bella at the school gates, not of J.J.

Detta shook her head. That wouldn't suit him. Us.

*

On the night bus home with J.J., when they finally got away from Bella's party, weight of a sleeping child in each of their laps:

I saw you, you know. She spoke low into the rumble of the bus, full of the jaded homeward-bound.

You did, did you?

Through the bus window the shuttered shops, winking lights, left behind.

What were you and Isabella so intimate about? You were whispering together for ages.

Uh-oh, here we go.

With her big tits you couldn't take your eyes off.

Can't we wait till we get home for this?

Reflected yellowish in the dirty window: her disappointed face.

And who phoned you, by the way?

Behind her own reflected face was J.J.'s.

No-one.

Yes, earlier. When we'd just arrived. I saw.

Truth was he was tired. All of her withholdings and her dramas of exclusion; sometimes it was just too much. And now this. He wanted to do things right, get home, put the children to bed, then tell her. Sit her down and tell her quietly. He was dreading it but prepared to do his best for her as always.

She turned to him. Don't put on the big sulk J.J., *please*. I'm just asking who you were on the fucking phone to?

Peter called, J.J. sighed. Resignation there, with just an edge of something malign, and also chemical, if he was honest. He'd admit that to himself much later, after she'd taken another sleeping pill and collapsed into their eldest's bed.

Why? she asked. For a second there was a shot of hope in her eyes.

Peter would never call them. So she knew why.

Naming Jimmy Wilde
Tony Curtis

The Tylorstown Terror

In the ring at the National Sporting Club in 1919
He shook the hand of the Prince of Wales,
Edward the Eighth to be,
'Good work, Jimmy, very well done,'
Having beaten Joe Lynch, a tough Irish-American,
After fifteen bloody rounds.
The hall heavy with cigar smoke,
The tiers of bow-tied gentlemen,
Polite applause, the ranks of toffs, Masons,
And cheering from the crowds outside in Covent Garden,
All for Jimmy.

Three years before, at Holborn Hall,
Young Kid Zulu, a New York Italian,
Went down in the Eleventh
And Jimmy became the Flyweight king of the world.

He took the morning train back to Wales
With the Belt wrapped in his suitcase,
Bought a farm, enlisted and served in uniform as a PT instructor,
One of the Famous Six, putting on shows for the Tommies.

Edward, Prince of Wales, the Welch leek in his cap,
Was still in uniform when he shook Jimmy's hand;
Twenty years later he would shake the hand of Adolf Hitler.

The Mighty Atom

In America they had no chance:
I knocked them all cold in America.

For months in 1919 from city to city,
Coast to coast, they were lining them up
And Jimmy, the champion, was knocking them down.

Then over again in '23, with Lisbeth that final time,
One more big pay day, his title at stake.
First Class: New York, on the Cunard *Aquatania*.
She'd carried the wounded back from the Dardanelles.

The young Filipino Pancho Villa beat him up,
Cut him down, a right hook he never saw,
At the Polo Fields on the Upper East Side
Where, three years before,
Ray Chapman of the Cleveland Indians
Was killed by a ball from the Yankees' pitcher Carl Mays.

The double-tiered stands and the bleachers were packed,
Up on Coogan's Bluff lights winked from the Mansions.
Jimmy's face hit the canvas and he stayed down in the Seventh.

In that ring, three months later,
Jack Dempsey, the Manassa Mauler,
Beat Luis Ángel Firpo, El Toro Salvaje de las Pampas,
A fight George Bellows would witness and then paint:
With Dempsey knocked out of the ring at the end of the First
To land next to the sketching artist.
Helped back in, he felled the bull in the Second.

Pancho was really Francesco Guillado, out on the Town
For two days after the fight, leeches, cronies and hoods
His companions, Miss New York on his arm.
Hot summer nights in the Bronx
With a stench coming from the streets
And not a breeze off the East River.
But nobody painted that.

The Ghost with a Hammer in his Hand

Today under the low winter sunshine
Jimmy lies with Lisbeth in the Barry Cemetery

A little old man beaten senseless by yobs
At Cardiff Station waiting for the last train.
He never came back from that low blow.

Fifty years before he would have seen them off,
Knocked them out cold one by one,
Stopping for a cuppa and starting up again
Under the fairground lights, bare-knuckled,
Making more in a night than a week in the pit.

You have to search for his plot, just grass
With a simple, faded marble headstone.
In this section the roots of the pines tilt the graves;
The shadows are long, the ground is uneven
And seems to move and feint as you get close.

Capital Vices
Conor Montague

Mark gulps down the remainder of his third Guinness. He places his empty pint glass to one side of its coaster and circles a crossword clue a third time. His glass is plucked from the table.

'Another pint?'

Mark remains engrossed in his crossword for a moment before glancing up at the bartender.

'Please.'

Mark returns to the crossword. The bartender's red Converse trainers remain stationary, vivid against the drab carpet.

'What are you stuck on, then?'

'Not stuck, just can't recall the answer.'

'If the clue is "definition of stuck," that's your answer right there.'

Mark puts down his pen, sits back, looks into moist mismatched eyes. Sculpted eyebrows are set at indifferent, the right one pierced with a silver hoop that reflects the stacked glasses tucked into her right shoulder.

'Deadly Sins. Two words, seven letters and five, second letter is A.'

'Seven and five?'

'Yes. Second letter is A.'

'Capital Vices.'

'Capital Vices?'

'Pride, greed, lust, envy, gluttony, wrath and sloth. The seven deadly sins, also known as capital vices.'

She leans into Mark and whispers.

'The sins which lead to ruination.'

She straightens and strides towards the bar, Mark's gaze following her. He turns back to his crossword, catches a flash of lilac through the half-light of the arched entrance to the bar. Tilt of her chin. The swish and bluster of her gait. Mark is fifteen, back at St Andrew's, enduring detention by rain-streaked windows. Penelope squeezing in beside him on a slipstream of attitude, her ragged lilac scarf a streak of cheer through the drab afternoon.

'Are you going to offer me a seat?'

'Penelope. Sorry, off in my own world.'

'Simone, Mark. My name is Simone.'

'What? Of course, Simone. What did I say?'

'You said Penelope. Thought the least I could expect is that you'd know my name after eight months.'

'Sorry babe, don't know what I was thinking.'

'Who's Penelope?'

'What?'

'Penelope. Who is Penelope?'

'I don't know any Penelope. Must have heard the name somewhere.'

'Why are you blushing?'

'I'm not blushing.'

'Yes, you are. Bright red.'

'I am now. Because you said I was blushing.'

Mark stands, reaches into his pocket.

'Want a drink?'

Simone stares for a moment, milking the last of the interrogation. She sheds a damp cream Macintosh and throws it over the back of a chair. Scarf a sleek guppy's tail over right shoulder, lips and eyelids tinted to match, black pencil lines and long lashes stark against alabaster skin stretched taut across sharp cheekbones by her grimace.

'Yeah, go on, I need one after the day I've had.'

'Gin and tonic?'

'Have you ever known me to drink anything else?'

'Just being polite.'

'I'm just thankful you remembered.'

Amber spotlight pierces the soft cotton of Simone's blouse. A man ogles from a high-stool perch, grey suit skewed on simian frame, tight across shoulders with cuffs a third of the way up long sinewy forearms. He turns a dented face to Mark as the bartender places a Guinness on the counter beside a gin and tonic.

'You alright, mate?'

'Alright. You?'

'Couldn't be better, mate.'

He nods towards Simone.

'Fit bird your missus.'

'Yes, she's very attractive.'

'Married?'

'Not yet, no.'

'You're engaged then?'

'I don't know if ...'

'Cause I don't see no stone.'

'No, well ...'

'Not too happy with you, mate.'

'Actually, we're very happy, couldn't be happier if you must know.'

'Don't mean no offence, mate, just making conversation.'

Mark picks up the drinks and turns from the bar.

'Well, if you'll excuse me.'

Mark places the drinks in front of Simone. He drags his chair around and sits to obstruct the view.

'Tough day?'

'Don't talk to me.'

'Adam?'

'The man hasn't a clue. What is it about managers?'

It's not just the lilac scarf. Those olive-green eyes, and her face. Is it the make-up? Not just: the oval shape, the pert nose, in a certain light she could pass. How had he not noticed?

'Are you even listening to me?'

'Course I'm listening.'

'You're off in your own world.'

'Just thinking how you're wasting your talent with that crew, Adam's never going to take you seriously.'

'I know. Can you believe he said that?'

'The man hasn't a clue.'

'It's insulting that's what it is, being objectified in that way.'

A waifish flame-haired woman in egg-yolk dungarees wrestles a house burger in an alcove behind Simone. She catches Mark's eye with mouth at reptilian stretch. Sauce-soaked burger tongue pokes through bread lips as she bites, spurting mayo over her fries.

'Where did you go to school?'

'As in secondary school?'

'Yes.'

'Why do you want to know?'

'Just curious.'

'Ealing Comprehensive.'

'All Girls?'

'Mixed.'

'Uniform?'

'Yes.'

'What was it like?'

'I don't know. Like any other school I suppose.'

'The uniform. What was the uniform like?

'Navy skirt – pleated – white blouse, red tie, blazer. Why?'

'No reason?'

'There's always a reason.'

'Just thinking maybe we could spice up our love life a little.'

'I wasn't aware it needed spicing up.'

'It doesn't. You know what I mean. Try something different.'

'I told you before, I'm not doing that.'

'Not that. I was thinking more of, you know, a little role play.'

'Role play?'

'With your uniform.'

'What are you, a paedophile?

'Of course not. Schoolgirls can be eighteen you know.

'Schoolgirls can be eighteen, Mark, but I'm thirty-one in case you haven't noticed. And you're thirty-four.'

'It's only a bit of fun.'

'It's bloody perverse, that's what it is.'

'You'd still pass for eighteen.'

Simone swells slightly and flicks hair from her forehead. She looks over her glass at Mark.

'That's not the point. It would be weird.'

'What's weird? We're consenting adults.'

'Let's just drop it, okay.'

'Okay.'

'I need another drink. You want a pint?'

'Please.'

Simone scrolls as she waits at the counter. The suited man leans towards her and speaks. She turns, finger poised on screen. He stands to shake her hand, forcing her to disregard the phone, then sits back down and passes a comment. She giggles, leans in with a retort as the drinks arrive. His pyroclastic guffaw cuts through the bustle like the deep urgent woofs of a startled Labrador. The man retrieves his wallet from the bar, extracts a card and hands it to her. She places it on her phone, puts both into her handbag, adds tonic to her gin and grabs both glasses, flashing a smile as she turns from the bar. It still plays on her lips as she places drinks on coasters and sits.

'What did he say?'

'Who?'

'The gorilla at the bar.'

'Stewart. He's nice.'

'Stewart?'

'He's a fashion consultant.'

'Fashion consultant?'

'You just going to repeat everything I say?'

'No, it's just that...'

'What?'

'He looks more defendant than consultant.'

'He thinks I look younger too.'

'Course he does.'

She leans across the table, kisses him on the lips, lingers eye to eye with hand cupped around his neck.

'Is my little baby jealous of the strange man at the bar?'

'Why would I be jealous?'

Moist juniper lips, waft of dried raindrops, black strands clinging to the white of her neck. Mark draws her to him, teasing and probing until she commits to the kiss. Three striped shirts with beer bellies enter on a cool tobacco breeze.

'Oy, get a room why don't ya?'

The men snigger as they pass. Simone picks up her drink and swirls the ice with her finger.

'You really think I'd pass for eighteen?'

'Told you I did.'

'So, you agree with Stewart?'

A smirk creases her left cheek. Mark wipes his lips with the back of his hand and places the pint to one side of its coaster.

'On this single occasion, I agree with Stewart, or to be precise, Stewart agrees with me.'

'Stewart agrees with you?'

'Let's just say, to avoid any argument, that on the subject of your youthful looks and all- round hotness, Stewart and I are in complete agreement.'

She leans to him, nestling into his shoulder.

'You're a clown, Mark Jones, you know that.'

'A really sexy clown?'

'Just a clown.'

She kisses him.

'Okay, I'll do it.'

'You'll do it?'

'The schoolgirl thing, I'll do it. It might be fun.'

'Really? Tonight?'

'I don't have my uniform at the flat. I'm home Friday, how about the weekend?'

He kisses her earlobe, feels her leg quiver beneath his hand as he whispers.

'Penelope.'

Mark attempts to mop the blinding sting with his shirt sleeve. The bartender appears and hands him a dry cloth. She moves Mark's pint and paper to an adjacent table, picks up the empty lilac-smudged Slim-Jim, whips out a second cloth, wipes in a furious counter-clockwise motion, flicking nuggets of ice onto the carpet. She returns Mark's pint, placing it on a fresh coaster, and picks up the paper, perusing the crossword as Mark dabs around his neck and inside the front of his soaked shirt.

'Portend.'

'Sorry?'

'Seventeen across. A sign or warning that something momentous or calamitous is likely to happen. Portend.'

She drops the paper onto Mark's table.

'Finished with the rag?'

A futile rub to his crotch and Mark hands the cloth over.

'I'm Mark, by the way.'

'Clotho.'

'Clotho?'

'Greek. My Mother's from Athens'

Clotho tucks the rag into the belt of her apron and walks back towards the bar, gathering glasses as she goes. Mark looks after her, scans the room. The three striped shirts laugh and point, hunched into one another, midriffs quivering. The flame-haired woman in egg-yolk dungarees leans back into her alcove, pouring salt onto a ketchup splotch on her chest. Other customers feign interest in conversations or newspapers.

Mark returns to his crossword, fills in Portend. Almost complete. One final clue remains unanswered. Fifteen down. Six letters. The three fates of Greek mythology - Lachesis, Atropos and…. The C of Capital is the first letter, the O of Portend the third. He looks to where Clotho clinks glasses into a wash basket. A barely touched pint of lager glows from where Stewart had been. Clotho grabs it, empties the glass into the sink before adding it to the other empties and heaving the basket into the washer. She whips out her rag and wipes down the counter.

Two Poems
Hilary Watson

Hai

'Cruel race,' Grandfather says: the way they run towards
koi ponds with their children, point out flashes of scales

and globbing mouths, the way they run to street cats
in Onomichi, collect manekineko, and smile at requests

for directions; the way Bunny Island is both bunnies and chemical
weapon plants, the way they bow in the street, bow in the 7/11, bow

in the temples; the way there's no need for any words but 'hai',
the way they point to moss in an ancient cedar tableaux, say
'Mononoke,

Mononoke!' like the forest spirits are out, the way the Manchester
monks
gift us with vegan food, meditation, translate their sacred graveyard,

the way they take phone calls at the doors of shinkansen and are
amused
by our joy at sakura weeks past its prime, the way they won't leave

chopsticks in gohan, the way they run after you in the street with
umbrellas,
and how they house Monet's Waterlilies on 'art gallery island',

the way Nagasaki opens her arms to you, welcomes you whole.

Meeting Your Son
(for Isobel)

Even though the bypass is bleak and clarted in dog shit
and the street names are different on the maps and signs,

still, the slope back to Swansea station is more quaint
than the noontime ascent, before Adda lay sleeping

on my chest, before I whispered into his dreaming.
Touching nose to nose, felt his curling feet and toes,

unfurled his fists, stared into his fervent eyes;
transfixed by the unlikelihood of our meeting.

Intermission
Catherine Wilkinson

He pitches into consciousness. Waits, stills his breathing, and rubs his t-shirt over his chest as sweat cools upon him. Ludo can hear the wind. Always the wind whips in the West. Peak winter, it jitters the locals in its incessance. But it's not too strong just yet. Sounds as if he could make the trip to the mainland, if he chose. He checks his phone, six a.m. Ach, he misses his teenage-doss circadian rhythms, when he slept and slept. Resisting all bells and buzzers. Languishing. Not like a dying spider, but delicious dreamless oblivion. What's that dramatic French phrase for missing someone? Yeah, *tu me manques*. Not 'I miss you'. But 'you are missing *from* me, part of me'. This bit especially for his beloved sleep: 'you are essential to my being'. Lately, and even now, on the island, he jerks awake, his brain whirrs and re-winds, re-plays. And within minutes, the internal nag in relation to the duty of the daily swim. Best get it out of the way. His resolve weakens as the day progresses, his self-imposed obligation hanging.

Swigs of orange juice spiked with cayenne. The burn of the spice kicks his system. He spreads raspberry jam onto a stale croissant and tosses kibble for the dogs to catch. His cousin Henry's dogs, minding them in lieu of rent. He eats standing, leans against the redwood breakfast bar - felled on Henry's farm, knotted and whorled, not sanded but rough. He grabs a still soggy towel from in front of the dead fire. The room is both brackish and smoky. Particles on his tongue. It's high tide, at which the sea is twenty-five steps from the cobalt wooden door of the small house sunk into the white sand on the lip of the beach.

He has unwound since his arrival, but he does still count and measure. It soothes somehow, simultaneously gives purpose. He sniffs, tests the air. Curlew cry. Eerie, slightly manic notes. He stands at the little gunmetal gate and watches the waves. A grey sea today, molten graphite. The waves a bit 'jolly', the fisherman jargon raising a wry smile. He folds his boxers and t-shirt onto the gate. Naked swimming. Bold for him, even if there is no one about. Liberating also.

A jog to the water. Cold grains of sand squish between his toes. He clasps and jiggles his junk. The dogs trot along, jib, career away from the swash. Deep breath and a shudder and in he strides. He has taken the water temperature regularly - the Atlantic even in this protected bay is a not-so-sweet nine degrees. Every single time however, it shocks him. Freaking freezing!

His feet hurt. Brutal. Masochism. As he reaches thigh depth, his balls shrivel and retract, walnuts, gone for the day. His dick shrinks to a miserable button mushroom. Wading, tensed, he hits nipple height and submerges, bursts back up with a bellow of outrage which ricochets the cove.

Scalp icy tight, fighting brain-freeze, he begins to swim the width of the bay. Counting his strokes. Swim and count. The pain will ease by the time he hits fifty strokes, that's not bad. He keeps thrashing forward, a ropey sort of crawl. As he relaxes, he moves into his zone - an underwater breaststroke involving smooth limb movement, great propulsion, a long glide… a sense of peace, a feeling of being away, almost alien, off land, enveloped and held. The ultimate astringency, his body and mind purged.

One hundred-and-fifty strokes and he has reached the jetty end of the bay. He swivels and sees the current is wrong, the waves too choppy to swim against, so he does his sea-jog back. Bionic in the slow-motion it provokes, as in his recurrent dream of running. Each powerful stride clears a street, a field. Soaring, close to flight.

Two more widths in the same manner and he is out, running up the beach while the three dogs corkscrew about him. Oyster catchers scatter, scuttle and squeak like clockwork toys. His feet thud like wooden blocks, numb and clumsy. The north wind is an utter bitch, not rewarding his efforts at all, an assault on his still naked body as he follows the crescent of the high-water mark, slipping in sand now shifting and sugary.

Yep-yep, it's worth it. This post-swim high will sustain him for the rest of the day. Muscles stretched, eyes stinging, skin smarting. Twenty minutes' investment for an endorphin boost of seriously behemoth proportions.

Further down the sweep of the bay, he sees the silhouette of a heron. Crane, according to the fishermen. Hunched, grumpy, dagger of beak. The bird unfolds, unfurls its long reptilian neck, lifts and flies, issuing its croak of alarm.

Next decision: shower or no shower. The collected-rainfall water supply, whilst sometimes annoyingly plentiful, still needs to be treated with care. He's also read that the immune system benefits of a cold start are negated by the scalding shower he craves. The only antidote to icy immersion, without it, his very bones remain cold for the day and he shivers regardless of the number of layers he rolls on. He does like however, the feel of sea salt crunchy upon his skin. So today, he settles for a savage head rub reminiscent of the childhood ear burnings inflicted if his hearty father was assigned hair-wash night.

The island is empty so soon in the year. He monitors though, sends out his drone on its daily recce. Feels like both a bit of a tool and a super-spy. Not one tree, he notes. They cannot withstand the maritime wind, the saline toxicity. From the drone shots, he can see how the beach house nestles into the isthmus between the sage-green commonage and the larger land fragment. The erosive power of the ocean working at the front, and from the rear.

He requires a second breakfast. Burying his porridge gloop with chunks of sugar crystallised in the damp sea air. And maple syrup. And cream. Not sour yogurt, lots and lots of cream. Healthy, warming, stomach-lining oats, now well buried and disguised. He gobbles the sludge, tugs at the neck of his scratchy Aran jumper and decides. Boat before walk. Boots on. Island family lore: bare feet at all times except in the boat - to guard against splinters, fishhooks, and stale fetid water infecting even tiny cuts and grazes. Experience told.

Barefoot, *nungapair*, in Indian, so Ayah, his and Henry's paternal grandmother, repeatedly advised.

Crackling in waterproofs, he pulls the boat from its running mooring - warns the dogs not to jump until it is safely alongside the sloping pier - then they all drop in. He bails out with a red sandcastle bucket, presses the choke, yanks the lead of the motor, and sets off. He takes pride in these manly actions, and in 'his' boat, his wooden currach. He auto-checks the long cuboid oars are shipped secure, lying perpendicular. Just in case of engine failure. To think, the islanders relied only upon them for years and years, no engine. No money. But mighty fit men.

He scans for his lobster pots, just two out. He admits to tiring of shellfish. Spoilt brat. Brown crab, lobster, line-caught pollock - his omega levels should be robust. Might help his somewhat screwed concentration span with exams pending. He steers the boat close enough to stretch and grab the first rope, monitors the drift towards the rocks. He pulls up the lobster pot, already heavy, weighted further by the seaweed's drag. As it hits the side of the boat, he grasps the cage and heaves it in. Dammit. Only rough-backed green feeler crabs. Fine for lobster bait but not for a meal, mere scraps of sweet meat. He opens the trap door and one by one grabs each crab by a pincer and hurls it back into the sea. The last two, he drops to the timber floor, stamps on them and stuffs the debris into the bait net pouch. He returns the pot to the sea - avoids the trap of coils at his feet - chucks first cage, then rope, then float.

He motors to the vicinity of his second buoy. The currach tips as the dogs all place their front paws on one side of the gunwale to check out a diving cormorant. 'Hey, boys', the boat steadies as they return to sit on their plank seats. Perch like three giant parrots. The cormorant has not surfaced, the dogs still watch, listen, ears pricked. Perhaps some other creature below of which Ludo is unaware, deep in the abyss.

Orange buoy located and, better luck, tonight's feed. One gleaming dark blue lobster, crusher claw locked to the bar at the back of the cage. And a lashing, black, conger eel. Liquid evil. And man-oh-man, livid or what. In its confines it thrashes. Ludo does not risk the needle teeth, careful with himself and the inquisitive yet balking hounds, he holds the cage well over the edge of the currach before releasing the hook on the door. Swiftly pulling it back to retain his lobster prize, he watches the conger writhe and sink, malevolent.

Arctic terns dive. Tiny missiles. Their call is clipped and tight. How his bird-nerd status grows. 'Sea-swallows', the too-soft local name. Auk Island looms with its 'Lord of the Rings' cliffs. Not possible to moor the boat at Auk, he has only once anchored and swum to its jagged edge. The dogs shift as the currach rolls in the swell. This patch of sea is choked with little brown jellyfish. Like floating toadstools. An anomaly, the sea temperature still low. Dunno what species either. Lion's-mane jellyfish have been invading the coast, maybe these are the young. The adults are huge. Great globules, sweeping amber tendrils. The sea now reminds him of school canteen mulligatawny soup. Buzzkill on all levels. Mind you, this mass of mini sea jellies might well tempt the mackerel into island waters relatively early in the year. That would make a tasty change of rations. He's tried cockles, way too bouncy. Islanders had, in bad winters, resorted to stew of crow flesh. Uh, nope. He's evolved an avatar-inspired homage to his various prey: the acknowledgement of debt, gratitude, the re-cycling of energy. But yeah, smoked mackerel with horseradish mayo, and some gooseberry jam.

Although the angle of the prevailing wind is not ideal and - he gauges, it's stiff, getting up considerably - he decides to check out the seal colony. Sometimes the cap of a seal pops up out of the water, the mammal curiously tailing his currach. There is a sheltered inlet of rocks however, where they collect for a nap and play time. Henry says the seals come out of the water to digest their food and to moult. 'Henry says'. Same age as his brother but more approachable, he's so comfortable in his own skin, it makes it easier to, anyway.... As he approaches the herd, Ludo cuts the engine, coasts. The crescent is packed with seals. Some in the water, some swooping beneath the boat. Many snooze fat-to-bursting upon the rocks. Long white whiskers. Some speckled or leopard in pattern, many steely-grey.

He and the dogs stand in the currach, drifting, fascinated. Shiny black eyes follow them. Abruptly, the Labrador, Java, launches himself into the water. What the… why? The seals could turn on him, attack him. Not wishing to scare any animal further or raise the temperature of the incident, Ludo does not shout - but watches as Java swims towards a bull seal lolling on a ledge but now very much awake. A strong swimmer, Java is wag-wagging his thick tail, his trade mark trick - a blend of rudder, propeller and glee.

Ludo dithers. Considers both a report of disaster to Henry, hell no, and jumping in himself, belatedly grabs the spaniel - when Java senses that this is not perhaps his very best adventure. He starts to paddle in a curve away from the big-boss-seal and back towards the boat, Ludo softly beseeching, begging. Once beside the currach - quick-quick, dogs can't tread water - Ludo grabs Java's scruff. Big, wet, dog, some heft - he hauls, one, two, gets an arm under Java's ribcage, and the two of them collapse backwards into the ribs of the boat. He breaks the dog's fall, gets trodden on by all three relieved tail-waving animals for his pains. Java violently shakes himself. Sheepishly begins to lick his coat dry. Dumb-ass dog, supposed to be antidote animals, not more bloody trauma. Ludo pats him, then turns the currach for home.

Licking. Licking wounds. School syllabus schmaltz, the Persian poet Rumi: 'the wound is the place where the light enters you'. He flicks his head, curses. A teenage scoff-reflex not completely wholehearted. So very self-aware, for all the good it's doing him. He believes he has managed to compartmentalise the night in Berlin. Block it out. He's trying really hard - focuses upon the elements, the lunar rhythms of the tides, physical tasks. The full *she*-bang. The currach bucks as he concentrates upon hitting the waves bow on. Rises, smacks the water, drops.

On return, he looks up seal facts on his phone, sitting on the highest mound of the commonage to get a signal. Evolved from large canine or bear-like creatures that returned to the water at some stage in Darwinism. Historically known as 'sea-dogs'. That might account for Java's leap, some genetic flash-back or affinity vibe? Not quite so dumb. Nevertheless, misguided - for he reads on that a shooting dog was killed, devoured, by seals. Trying to retrieve a bird. And, jeez, the teeth of seals are serrated and hooked backwards so that once bitten, it's almost impossible for a victim to escape.

He decides to dwell no further on the incident, heads to the Atlantic side of the island. More rugged. Sharper rocks. Bigger sky, exposed. A harder, stronger wind. It's picked up significantly, a vicious squall. Wild and noisy sea, its suds spattered and cast far inland. He scrambles over deep layers of rock fragments. Bones in a dinosaur burial pit.

Nungapair once more, fingers and toes gripping, he climbs a huge single rock, and stands up cautiously, tests his balance. The offing's blurred, the vast space... dilates his mind. He leans his long frame at a forty-five-degree slant on the rock edge, slopes into the power of the gale, allows it to hold his weight. Arms outstretched, hair ripped back, his eyes streaming.

Three Poems
Linda McKenna

Self-Portrait in Silk

I dress myself in shattered silk,
allow the tattered ribbons fragment
further, alternate iron-embedded
deepest mourning, with bloody
tang of ballroom pink, take solace
in salt-encrusted, wedding white.
I will not abandon it for sturdy cotton
but relish its abrasion, how the metal's
razor teeth worry fissures into rips,
until embrittlement is complete.
I accept the swirling dust cloud
of thread I scatter, study how the weft
disappears first, the warp, always
stronger holds its own for longer.

My Son, At War

I have ordered winged victory,
banded with brass to prevent
the wood from bruising; inside
not velvet but baize and tooled
leather, the drawers run smoothly,
the slope is gentle, nibs are sharp,
a bank note is tied up with a red
ribbon. You have heard my litany,
eat properly, dry clothes thoroughly.
I know you will not be careful.

So, look inside the pocket
of your overcoat and find
a packet of skeleton keys,
their bows are curled,
crown, kidney, heart.

Trompe l'Oeil

There's not enough red for a huntsman's
coat, nor enough pink for a ballerina's

skirt, so I settle on a peacock; the blues
have faded in patches, so the feathers

will not mimic the symmetry of nature.
But it will cover up the gaping hearth,

draw the eye; become a talking point.
Someone will remember the peacocks

of his childhood, on an estate he ran
away from, someone else the symbol

of Jesus or the aggressive male, the modest,
brown-winged female; and of course,

vanity. And then, the skill of the stitcher.
If the colours aren't as vibrant as they

should be, this is not science, nor art,
just the sleight of hand we need these days.

A Suitable Feast
Cath Barton

Apparently I'd been recommended to her by a mutual friend. I didn't ask who.

'My name,' she said, 'is Angélique.' I couldn't place her accent.

The meal, she told me, was to be a re-enactment. She pronounced the four syllables separately and carefully. Then paused. Perhaps, I said to my husband afterwards, she was expecting a reaction, wanted one even. All I did was raise my eyebrows when she explained, but of course she couldn't see that over the phone.

'In your house?'

She gave a high little laugh, as if that was a stupid thing to say, but perhaps she was just relieved I hadn't asked more probing questions.

No, she said, her house was far too small. It would be in a little community hall. I might have seen it as I drove out of town, on the left of the main road just down a lane. It was, she said, fully equipped, and there was plenty of parking. It was the devil's own job finding space for visitors to park in her road, the neighbours didn't like it. She was gabbling, but I just let her carry on.

I suspected that 'fully equipped' meant the hall had a couple of electric rings, maybe a small oven. I told her I would do all the cooking at home beforehand. And bring my own crockery and cutlery. All part of the service.

'So long as there are tables I can push together,' I said.

'Of course,' she said, laughing again in that nervous way. 'And you'll bring tablecloths?'

I assured her I would provide everything she needed, and of good quality. Asked her to email me details of the food she wanted, any special dietary requirements. As for any meal booking I took. I put the date in my diary. It was a Thursday in late March. Plenty of time for me to do my research, practice any dishes with which I was unfamiliar. I just hoped there wouldn't be snow when the time came. Even lanes just off the main road out of town get blocked so easily.

So many of us have had to turn our hands to something new. It was an obvious choice for me. Something I was good at. Something I could enjoy. Something to take my mind off the losses. I was lucky, had stayed well, at least physically. On days when I woke with anxiety sitting on my chest I got up and baked. I could never make too much bread, now that I had the business. I was surprised, at first, how quickly it took off.

'Your food's good,' my husband said. 'You shouldn't be surprised.'

I got on with it. It occupied my hands, and I needed that.

Angélique and I agreed the menu by email. Warm food for the main course, not hot. That would have been the way things were on the original occasion.

'And no lamb,' she wrote in her message. 'Pope Benedict XV has told us they didn't eat lamb – it was before the time of ritual slaughter.'

I didn't argue, it wasn't my place as the hired help, no matter what I believed. I suggested we make all the food vegetarian.

'One less thing for you to worry about,' I said in my email.

'Am I worried?' she typed in her reply, followed by a string of emojis that gave me the impression she was feeling jittery about the whole thing.

'Trust me,' I wrote. 'It will be a suitable feast.'

Two weeks before the agreed date she rang again.

'Did you want to change something?' I said.

No, no, it wasn't that, just that she'd forgotten to mention that there would be music.

I sat down. Music? But– 'That won't be a problem for you, will it? I thought we'd have some before the meal, and then after they've eaten the main course. You could lay out the sweet things on a side table, ready for them to help themselves.'

What kind of music? I knew before she said it. Wondered then about the mutual friend. Who must surely know about my previous life, if she – I'd assumed it was a woman, men don't think about catering, at least not organising it – was a proper friend.

She said it was like a guitar, but quieter.

'Yes, I know what it sounds like,' I said, trying to keep my voice steady. 'It won't be a problem for me. Actually it'll be lovely. Lovely for the diners.'

I felt everything you would expect me to feel – pain, grief, jealousy. Fury on top of all that. That someone would be doing the job I wanted, the one I would have done, the one I should have done, while instead I sat in a little kitchen behind a closed door like a scivvy. Well, I wouldn't. I would ring back and tell her I couldn't do the catering after all. Invent an excuse. I'd wait a day and do that.

Of course I didn't. Apart from anything else I would lose too much money. I told myself to get over it. When I woke with crushing anxiety I got up and baked. I tried out all the dishes for the meal on my husband. He liked them, all except the bitter herbs. Bitter isn't a taste most of us like. But it was necessary for this meal.

One week before the appointed date we walked by the river, my husband and I. There was a breath of warmth in the air and sprays of white blossom on some of the trees. I knew it was a bad sign, this midwinter spring. The cold would come back. Back home I made soup. When I was dishing it up I spilled some and cursed. My husband raised his eyebrows but didn't say anything.

On the day of the supper we woke to a yellowish light. Snow had fallen overnight. Our street filled with the shouting of children delighted to have the day off school. I got on with what I had to do for the meal. I'd bought all the food and prepared most of the dishes already. I'd made hummus, baba ganoush and a bean dish. I'd macerated dried figs in olive oil and honey, ground nuts and mixed them with chopped dates for a charoset. My kitchen smelled of cinnamon and saffron. I just had the flatbreads to to make and little pies.

I was weighing out the flour when Angélique rang, fretting as I knew she would about the weather.

'Don't worry,' I said. 'Everything's under control. And our car is a 4x4. No problem getting to the hall.'

I looked out of the window. 'Actually, the snow's melting here already.' I hadn't asked her how her guests were going to get to the hall and I didn't do so now; that was her problem, not mine.

'Okay. Yes. Good. Fine. But there's a problem. The lutenist lives up a valley somewhere in the middle of Wales. She's just rung me. Says the roads are impassable. I don't suppose you know anyone who–' Her voice tailed off.

I suppose I must have been quite sharp with her. My husband said I was. I didn't care. Told her she'd better sort out a CD player if she wanted music.

The snow had all but gone by 5pm, and I packed everything into the car and set off for the hall. I passed two men in swinging loden coats walking along the road, wheeling small suitcases behind them. I glanced in my rear-view mirror and knew – was it by the way they walked, their self-assurance? – that they were heading for the hall, for the feast. I would have stopped and offered them a lift, but the car was full of food.

Several of the other guests had already arrived, filling the space with their luggage and effusive greetings, talking of hold-ups and relief at getting there in time.

'I would have absolutely hated to let Angie down,' I heard one saying.

The loden coats arrived with stamping on the doormat and hellos to Pete and Tom and Matt and Nate. And all the others, all the names I expected. Angélique hadn't given me a guest list, but I didn't need one of course.

'Put your bag in here, Jude,' she said to one of the loden coats.

I tried not to stare, but when they were all seated at the row of tables pushed together and I brought in the wine I got a good look at him. There was, of course, nothing to mark him out.

I'd told my husband about it, this re-enactment idea of Angélique's.
'What, the whole thing?' he'd said.
'Don't be daft. It's just a meal. A bit of fun. She said it was her son who asked for it. That it would be a way of bringing all his old university friends together. None of them have seen one another these past two years.'
'And his name is– no, let me guess.'
'Actually, she hasn't told me his name.'

He'd been ill, she'd told me. Was better though. A good deal better. All the more reason to indulge him with this treat. He'd travelled in the Middle East, loved Levantine food. There'd been a girl he'd met there. They'd been together for a while. He'd heard somehow that she was in England now, tracked her down. They'd talked on the phone and he'd wanted to invite her too.
'I dissuaded him. Told him it wouldn't be the right time. And anyway, it wouldn't have been authentic. It was just men, wasn't it, at the supper?'
And that was how she'd set it up, her son in the middle of the table and his male friends alongside him, six on the left, six on the right. And left us to it.

Afterwards the police sent someone to interview me. Did I have any suspicions? she asked. About the man called Jude? Or anyone else? I told her I hadn't. That they were a group of young men like any other, in my experience. Which admittedly was limited. That everything had gone to plan with the meal. That it had been a success, as far as I knew. Of course, from the kitchen I couldn't hear what was said, and much of the conversation was drowned by the recorded music. I hadn't heard any raised voices. Perhaps, I said, someone had turned up the volume at the crucial moment, because usually lute music was very soft, that was the beauty of it.

I'd cleared up after the meal, after everyone had gone. The mess was no more than average. I didn't mention the spilt wine. Wine stains were not unusual either. I knew how to get them out of tablecloths. Not that the policewoman was interested in that. No, I didn't know where they'd gone after the meal, that wasn't my business. My job was to clear up, lock the hall and leave the key in the safe place I'd been told about. Which I'd done. Yes, it had been snowing again when I left. And yes, I'd been paid. The money had been sent by bank transfer the next morning. By whom, she asked? By Angélique, I said, the woman who'd hired me, the mother of the unfortunate young man. Well, I'd assumed it was her. Who else would have sent me that exact sum?

I was sorry, I said, that I couldn't be of more assistance.

Someone contacted me from one of the newspapers. I told them I had no comment. The report they published contained (in my opinion) sensationalist and unnecessary details about how the young man had died, to say nothing of ridiculous claims about the meal. It said I'd served roast lamb, and that the guests had 'torn it apart with their bare hands.' Which any of those present could have told them was not true. Quite apart from lamb being unsuitable for the feast.

Three Poems
Jackie Gorman

The Heart Dreams of Being an Iberian Hare

The day I left my
husband, my heart was
dreaming of
being an Iberian Hare in Spring.

Standing upright and wide
eyed in a Verdial olive grove
with its fists cutting through
the air.

The arteries and aorta turning
quickly to shades of ginger,
russet and black fur on the
spine.

The mitral valve with
its tapered cusps
became
a twitching curious nose.

A creature full of
oxygen, instinct, blood
and life.
It made a faint purring sound.

For a moment it was a
hare, alive and thumping
hard,
its hind legs tapping out a signal.

Then it became shy and hid
again for a long time in the
form of flattened grasses in my
chest.

Placing my trust
in language, I lay
down in its tight
embrace.

A Vision of Your Saxon Grandmother in Laos

In the Talat Sao Shopping Centre in Vientiane, I see your Saxon Grandmother carrying a large tray of eggs. Oma disappears down a warren of small alleys, weaving between market stalls selling fish, mobile phones, apricots and charcoal. I'm sure it's her but I can't find her again in the glare of the sunlight. I remember the first time you showed me an image of her, projected onto a Tipperary wall from your slide deck of old photos. She was reaching out to grab an egg that rolled from her table in the Ore Mountains. Years later, at the corner of my eye, I saw you as a boy in this Laos market reaching up to grab the outstretched old hands in front of you.

The Museum of Natural History in my Mind

Sometimes I forget it exists and then I hear the hum of Dragonflies flapping their wings in my spinal cord. Usually, the first thing I notice is a dinosaur egg in my brain stem. Faint shades of rust and teal run across the rugged shell. Then I notice a Blue Whale in my cerebellum. Hungry for krill and carrying a calf, she is stranded and alone. Near my amygdala there's a fossil of a Pterodactyl. Its wing spread out to fly through limestone. Teeth biting down on once caught fish. A skull of a Manatee is stuck in my frontal lobe. The lush sea grasses float just out of reach. A Black Bear from the Adirondacks appears at the Sylvian Fissure, then lumbers past with sunshine on its back. Large paws outstretched and claws unfurled. It smells musky and sweet. All of these things speak of life. How an embryo found its place in a womb, how some things learnt to breathe underwater or grew to love the comfort of the herd or hibernation when the air smelled of frost. How they learnt to eat and sleep. This means my brain holds fur, water, bone and claws. It has a constant sound. It smells of blood and life. When I lie down on the grass, I can hear it singing itself into being. My tailbone twitches.

A Letter of Sorts to Dylan Thomas
Órfhlaith Foyle

Dear Dylan,

There you sat in the pub, your face all curled up in smoke and you wanted me to smile. I said my smile was worth more than any of your boy poems. You said I suited the green juice of your poems, that I am the well-behaved sister of your mad girl. Well I told your mad girl that I wasn't having any of your slobber on my bed and she laughed and said now why would he like your kisses?

You drank from my beer. You asked for a cigarette, lit and God forgive me, but I opened my mouth to inhale you. Pub voices rolled behind our backs and your eyes looked at mine.

'You've been in love with me for years,' you said and stroked a fleck of beer from my chin.

'Years,' I agreed and gazed at your pudgy smile.

I magicked you up, dear Dylan to have this conversation. I went back in time and through all your poems to find you here, perched solid on a bar stool, smelling sour from the previous night and you've known how many times I have thrown your poems against the wall, your dominion-less deaths and your Fern hills.

And you said you didn't mind where I had blown in from because I bought you a beer and gave you a few cigarettes.

'A poet,' you said. 'Really,' you said.

And you sounded like those taunts in my head.

Well, I am just as good as you, Dylan Thomas and I'll prove it too.

We were sitting in that pub and I told you that not much has changed between our worlds. There's a war at the moment, not exactly world war three, but it began in Europe too. Stalin and Hitler are dead but there's another version now and the bombs can fly for long stretches by themselves before they obliterate buildings with people in them, and refugees, there are always refugees…and what is the point of life, I asked you.

'I don't know,' you said.

Then Caitlin broke free from her American airman, pushed in between us, grabbed your head and kissed it. You growled, shook her grip off, took her by the neck and forced her to look at me and said.

'Say hello to this poet, my love.'

Caitlin plucked my cigarette and put it in her mouth.

'Cat got your tongue?'

'No, he's got my knee.'

Caitlin's Airman sauntered up. 'Can I buy you all a drink?'

He was tall in a white lemonade way, straight lined with straight lips and straight eyes. He ordered new beers and of course you cajoled a cigarette from him.

'Can't take you anywhere,' Caitlin said with her eyes on me then just as cool she smiled up at her airman who whisked her off to dance. She was all legs and knickers. Dust raised from the pub floor and men watched from their beer glasses. Women too.

You said, 'Let's shuffle forth, you and I.'

'No.'

You gave me that smile that your mother never stopped loving.

Your mother didn't like me, did she? She said what sort of woman are you to gallivant down here with my son and his wife and child absent? I told her that her lovely son and I wander about the bomb sites in London, researching for his film work. My work too.

'She writes a few words here and there, Mam.'

'Does she,' asked your father. 'Have I heard of you?'

'Not likely,' you said.

'Unpublished,' I said.

Your father asked me about my family and you said I was an orphan.

'They drowned together,' you said. 'A lover's knot.'

They hadn't. I told you a story they had died quite normal deaths, one after the other, one from influenza and the other from a heart attack, five years apart and so far gone from me, I hardly thought of them except in bed at night when sounds from the street made me lonely and afraid, made me a little girl again thinking of death.

You listened to my work and said 'You have good phrasing. Good rhythm here and there so I suppose you are a poet in your own right.'

'You said something similar to Lynette Roberts, didn't you?'

'When did I?'

'I don't know. Maybe when you were late for her wedding.'

I had written something about walking in a field back home. I had used words my parents had said. *The soft stare of a brown mouse in the dried grass. The fox high-stepping it in the top field. A slew of starlings. The sun baking your backbone until your arse is blazing.*

You said my words were too simple. I went too much for the image of the thing rather than the sound. And no girl poet should ever use the word 'arse'. And what about rhyme you said with your put on accent, your Welsh 'Rrrrrr, I said.

'Too much love in that poetry of yours,' you said. 'A female poet is what you are. You don't have the men's vigour. None of you do, mind.'

I wanted to hit you. You and any other.

'I have bloody vigour,' I said.

You giggle and turned to watch Caitlin dance. I thought this is where I am, in a pub sniping with Dylan Thomas. I thought of all the characters I could have picked and this is him and me.

Then you sly-ed your gaze back to me.

'So a lonely cold bed and page for you now, is it?'

'It's a fine bed and a fine page ,' I said. 'I have a desk against the window. I see all the crows and cats and dogs.'

You put your head close to mine and I saw your pink scalp beneath your pretty curls.

Your Caitlin told me that you'd smother me in the end.

I told your mad-girl of that damn attic that I didn't need any of your dark Welsh wind and running words. I have my own words.

'Cat's got your knee,' you whispered.

My eyelids squeezed themselves as you leaned in and kissed my forehead. The briny days old unwashed smell of you. I thought of the colour of your underpants. Probably some colour beyond any other. Your lips big and baby pink and your tongue licked my damp forehead.

'Sherbet.'

I think. I think. I think I need to clutch at your jacket, Dylan feel its old wool made smooth by you and perhaps your father or someone you might have stolen it from. I need to clutch it. I need to steady my brain from falling into a dark room at the back of my mind after I read your poetry.

I need my own words.

I try steady the boiling in my head while you watch Caitlin dance among the American broth and brawn.

Bald headed youngsters with death crow eyes and muscles in their thighs.

I hear your voice in my head.

'Put that in a poem, mind.'

You smiled with that face your mother loved as I plucked the cigarette from your mouth and put it to the top of your head then into your mass of curls which flickered up one by one until you were a mass of brilliant flame, my male Medusa.

I've known of the girls you slept with, Dylan. Girls and sad women, rich women and lovers of your words. How they thrill to your rolling 'r's'. You mad girl told me that it's your arse they want rolling over them. That white blobby flesh slapping and settling into them or just onto them.

'He wants the cuddling type,' she said. 'Not yours. Not really.'

I am shrimp thin. Shrimp hard and brittle. A man clasped my upper arm one night and cooed at how it almost all fit into his fist. How lovely to break you in two, he had whispered and place you back together again, sliver by sliver. I didn't want to sleep with him and he tightened his fist about my arm. He said it served me right to know how it felt to have your neck and spine cracked to that inch above death.

I ran home to you and your poems.

Come sleep with me said the butterfly to the Cherry Blossom tree.

I burned you up, Dylan.

Your face lifted into ashes. Your curls frittered into air. Your words shuddered up through my legs and into my heart. Shelf dust, gas ring, kettle, cups, the very guts of the world seemed to vomit inside your poems. I thought of our bodies lifting upwards in the blast of your words then falling back down, all the bodies falling, all dying yet never dead.

Three Poems
Pauline Flynne

Mary of Egypt Walks into the Desert to Repent her Lascivious Life

I like this feeling, walking away,
gathering distance to where desert shrub
peppers the ground, how
a lone acacia tree shows itself for miles.

What I like about the acacia tree
is that I can rest in its shade
and sing with the choir of bees
humming in the canopy.

When I find honey from date palm
blossoms, I roll my tongue
into a tube and suck, suck, suck it in.

What I like about date palms
is that the fruit, plump, wrinkled
and sweet as caramel, gives me pleasure,
without expecting praise.

I search out moss on south sides
of boulders or under a bush,
sup up fog and mist
through the tips of its leaves.

What I like about desert moss
is that it quenches my thirst,
and does not impose a charge.

I'm watchful of wildlife, lions
and snakes, but sand cats can come close,
gazelles too. Sand cats, so independent,
their kittens, so inquisitive.

And what I like about gazelles,
stotting through long grasses
is that they bring theatre into my life,
with no need of applause.

When I lift my nose to the breeze,
the sharp scent of the samwa herb
draws me in, like a female to her mate.

What I like about the samwa plant
is that it keeps me well,
and does not look for payment.

I let my hair tumble to the ground
to cover me when I need to pray
or hide. When I am cold.

What I like about my hair is that it is mine,
it will grow and grow even after I die.

August

For five days there was a heat wave
in West Cork. Children splashed

about the pool, tomatoes and fruits
ripened in poly tunnels

beyond the view of the house,
at the end of the path, lined with tree fern.

I took the radio presenters' advice
and stayed under a garden umbrella.

Seven times I took a dip in the water,
seven times sun-screened my skin.

The dog lay tethered in the shade,
ears flicking lazy insects,

teenagers lolling about indoors
on their phones and tablets.

For more than three hours through rain
we drove across country.

Home, astilbe, pink and fluffy
as cotton candy when we left,

hung like limp seaweed on rocks.
Agapanthus lapis lazuli was in bloom.

And honeysuckle, crawling through trees,
scented the twilight.

Good Shoes

Every since we met outside the door
to our flats on Northbrook Road,
we've picked and unpicked
the small details of our lives.

Walking along Castletown beach,
or in Marley Park, your arms folded
if the subject is serious, your stride
a little ahead of mine, me bent
on keeping up, knowing your fast pace.
Chats about shoes recur: two-toned
grey leather, tartan ribbon or multi-
coloured laces, funky stitching.

Joy for the moment, then defeat
as pain begins, as your feet reject
the shape at the toe, a tightness
over the mid-foot, a scraping
at the heel and worst of all
your struggle with *Pes planus*.
Shoes are returned for a refund,
a credit note, or gifted to a friend.

I still trail you as you forge ahead
in shoes roomy enough for orthotics.
Aids to stop your feet from falling in.
You dreaming of comfortable footwear,
me wishing I'd trained as a shoe-maker.

Joy
Karys Frank

Eric was late to the airport, but Laura was not there yet with her life.

The pieces of it would not come together. She was studying, she was being evicted, she worried her boyfriend was cheating on her. Someone had stolen her identity and was buying blenders from abroad in her name and she had spent a lot of time sorting it out.

The police told her the blenders were likely bought for mixing drugs. How could people do that to their bodies? Laura was training to be a nutritionist.

He and Helen had raised a good person, Eric thought, even if Laura was a little highly-strung, but she would get there. The previous night he'd had a disturbing dream of Laura as a puppet, jerked about by unseen hands, wooden jaw dropping and snapping wordlessly, but he wouldn't tell Laura about it. He'd tell Helen.

Eric ran full tilt into the adamant fact of Helen's death.

Incredible, that Helen's body could be cold, under earth for two years. Eric resisted the urge, of course, to go to it straightaway.

But really, where *was* she?

Practised, he offloaded panic on a steady outbreath. He would never meet Helen again. This is normal. We're born and we live in a body that dies and then someone who loves us arranges to set it on fire, or has it put in a hole in the ground. He shouldn't find it strange.

Eric dropped onto a bolted-down plastic chair in the Arrivals lounge. He had trouble seeing the digital display due to his eyes being a little watery of late. Two carrier bags of M&S sandwiches and crudités rustled at his feet.

The chairs all faced the same way, as though nothing unexpected should happen behind the people seated, or to the sides. The grid formation comforted him. It curbed the impulse to be wayward.

Eric had heard that some people, when at the tops of buildings, feel an irrational urge to throw themselves off. Eric thought he knew this feeling. Although he didn't, not really. He'd never been depressed. Not stalked by the black dog.

But Eric recognised the impulse. A subversive drive to wreck what's good, in case it's going to get wrecked anyway, so you might as well get in there first. You do it; you jump, just to see.

It happened to be Eric's birthday. He practised showing delight at the sight of his daughter, extra delight because she was visiting on this day. He had to be careful, though, not to seem happier than she'd ever seen him. He planned to take a present from her with a kiss and a soft chiding. He'd say he hoped she hadn't spent too much.

Laura's flight from Newcastle was announced. Eric stood up. He put his glasses on, took them off again. He straightened himself, smoothed his Parka and tried to look like he wasn't missing anything. No, he'd never acted on that impulse to jump off a building. And that wasn't nothing. He took out a tissue to wipe his eyes, which were playing up. He waited to greet his only child, now an adult. He waited without her mother because her mother was dead.

Laura barely paused to hug Eric, but it was long enough for him to feel she'd lost weight. He thought to tell Helen, corrected his error, then wondered what Helen would have had to say about it, and what he should say about it to Laura, if anything.

They exited though the airport's hermetic doors to human-made scents. Espresso at a coffee stall, warm croissants, petrol from taxis and the vape fumes of tour guides awaiting groups. He looked around at these activities, at the strangers' industriousness and entrepreneurialism. He loved being alive.

The plan was for a picnic. In the park, he wasn't sure about sitting on grass. He worried he couldn't get up unaided. To his relief, Laura picked a bench. She insisted he roll up his sleeves to raise his vitamin D levels, while she applied factor fifty.

As Laura fished about in her bag, Eric sat back and mentally rehearsed again for the moment she would produce his present. But there was no present. Laure just pulled out an enormous black phone and jabbed at the screen. It was kicking off at home, she told her father. Some chancer had called at her door, according to her boyfriend, pretending to be a bailiff after her stuff. The sheer brass neck!

Secretly, Eric worried about the series of catastrophes that had entered Laura's life around the time she met her boyfriend. But honestly, what advice could he give about relationships? When he met Helen he'd kissed her early, sure in finding *this*. Yes *this, now*. And that had been that.

Eric looked around at the park. He noted the blossom on cherry trees, the pristine, white petals' ecstatic abundance. He inhaled the scent of cut grass. Even the smell was green. He missed Helen most when the seasons changed. When the life force of a season ebbed and nature regenerated into remarkable new forms.

So what if Laura had no present for him? It was Helen who'd kept them tethered to the rhythms and rituals of family life. Now it was just Eric and Laura, making their shaky ways forward. If that meant missing out on a new dressing gown, or an Amazon gift card, well.

Eric was pulling the lid off a pot of hummus when Laura shouted: 'Hey! Edie! Edie!'

Laura waved over her father's head to a young woman sunning herself some metres away. Edie waved back, raising her sunglasses.

'Oh my God!' called this Edie. 'Oh my God!'

It turned out that Edie and Laura had been school-friends. Eric didn't recall the name. He looked at Edie's face, trying to make out if she had become herself yet. Laura was not quite herself yet, but at her age this was normal.

As Laura scrambled items together, in readiness to leave him, Eric thought back to the school where he'd worked as a caretaker. Most pupils there had not yet become themselves either, apart from a rare few. Eric recalled polishing floors before students arrived in the churchlike building. He'd had a feeling, when light flooded in through the high windows, that he could not precisely name. He explained it to Helen as being, surely, the promise of the young people. But at such times, when the school gates opened and the pupils, with their giant bags, their larking and their shrieks, flowed past him, he'd had to cast down his face to not give himself away.

'I'm sorry, Dad, but it's Edie!' Laura left her father to talk to her friend. Eric watched Laura collapse to her knees in front of Edie.

Edie screamed and said again, 'Oh my God!' Eric watched a new energy consume Laura. She was excited, clearly happy, in a way she had not been with him.

'Don't worry about me, you two. You stay, you talk,' called Eric, waving his hand at the notion he might mind.

After a while Laura returned, said she was really sorry, but Edie was going through something.

'You enjoy being with your friend. I'll see you later.'

Eric smiled at her. Laura nodded.

She said, 'I fly back at seven.'

They made no plan to meet again.

He felt Helen would be pleased with him. He was freeing Laura to a fine day without him.

Eric should probably go home. But something in the air, maybe it was Spring, or the feeling of bounty all around, made him stop by the high street.

At the bookshop there were discounts. After browsing, he picked two titles, resisting a three-for-two offer and enjoying the rare feeling of discernment this gave him. These books had trashy-looking covers.

He imagined Helen's amused responses. Well, he was going to buy them anyway. Helen would look for books about heroes and heroines, about lives being saved against all odds, about last wishes being granted, about amazing coincidences, showing there was a plan after all, and that there was someone for everyone. Whereas Eric enjoyed seeing characters stray, then get corrected, or correct themselves, or not. He liked seeing how far it was possible to stretch a life before it breaks or snaps back and slaps you in the face. He would start reading again soon. When he had the ability to absorb a life outside his own.

On his walk to the bus stop, nothing bad happened. He dodged the cracks on his path, enjoying being the opposite of the man his father had raised him to be. As the bus pulled up, Eric considered that his father would never have taken a bus. Something to do with machismo, he guessed.

On the bus, people watched their screens, reverent. Eric studied closely the fixtures and fittings of the bus interior as though seeing them for the first time. He marvelled. Look at that! Every bolt, nut and plastic item designed, and made to fit perfectly into a greater entity.

That was when it started. He felt a familiar embarrassment, a spontaneous undoing. It was like a film of a mirror being smashed, in slow motion, playing in reverse. Scattered pieces came back *whoosh* to remake a whole. This hadn't happened since Helen's death, and now here, of all places… *harmony*.

He resisted the word. Was *harmony* right?

Helen was the only one he'd told. She had not known what to do with the knowledge that her husband experienced transcendent feelings, at random, when opening the dishwasher, or shaving, or putting away laundry.

She'd sensed that her husband had hit upon something, or learned an inarticulable secret, though she didn't know what, having never experienced transcendence herself.

The feeling held. Not on a bus, Eric prayed. These feelings could transmute, showing themselves in such damned physiological ways. A blood rush to the cheeks, a change in the eyes.

Eric tried to ground himself by thinking of the failings of words. How, at a funeral, people will say of the departed "he would do anything for anyone" or "she was a friend to all" while mourners worked to align these words with their experiences of the deceased. At Helen's funeral words reached for her, but fell short.

Eric's bliss subsided. The bus juddered and hissed. As always when weary, Eric became preoccupied with physical sensations. Warmth, a pleasurable stirring in his groin, his own hand on his cheek, mothering him.

Inside his coat, his palm moved to feel his heart's thudding. Helen had bought him a pulse tracker, after his spell in hospital. They'd joked about it racing during sex. Once, Helen confided, at climax Eric said something like *Jesus Christ*.

He ate the rest of the picnic in front of his TV. Room temperature tzatziki and bread fingers. How good it was to eat when hungry.

Seven o'clock passed. Nothing from Laura. Eric imagined the nose of the aircraft, ridiculous, comic book huge on the runway at Southend. He envisioned tiny Laura climbing into the fuselage and it taking off. How could such a thing be suspended? But these days, Eric was used to accepting impossible thoughts.

He went to bed. How good it was to sleep when tired.

He thought back to the hospice, when the nurse told him that Helen's eleventh-hour vivacity was common, that 'there's sometimes a Lazarus moment,' when a dying person becomes lively, before the end. He wished the nurse had said it earlier. For Helen to be so splendidly herself, just before he lost her, was a cruel thing.

Eric tried to picture Helen, but couldn't think where she was.

So preoccupied was he imagining Helen, and checking for a message from Laura, he didn't take his pill.

Dawn broke on a morning without clouds. In this state he neither slept nor was awake, because of the exhilaration in his heart, and his anticipation of the coming day.

Three Poems
Jane Lovell

Perhaps the Crow

Perhaps it was the crow that unseamed the mountain that day, its
three bleak warnings, or its curse, the mountain a negative,
manmade, not for any purpose but amassing its own unwantedness.

> Hold a strip of celluloid
> to the light: peaks of white land
> divide a black sky.

See the crow catch the light, its sheen white to the artist's eye, oil on
his blade. Mark its swagger, its tilt and bead-eye considering.

> He knows the welling
> of the springs,
> the Earth's instability.

He keeps his distance while they dig out the bodies, small and
unfolded, the place where there should have been fields and trees
having shed the weight of decades.

> Tons of shale and soil,
> a tidal wave.

How do we paint the heart of a man who refused his child to stay
home, her cheeks pink as they were with fever? And it being a half
day before the break.

Walls and desks shuddering,
glass snapping.

In the chapel, how the light is changed, air smelling of earth. Between
the pews, wet slabs, grit underfoot. Disturbing the space: women
cleaning faces, cloths and clanking buckets. Outside the commotion
of industry.

She is here.

No one knew how cold
the air could be.
How endless.

Doll face, filthy hands and clothes. Arms hang like wings as he holds
her. Head lolls. Lips part, black.

Perhaps an omen,
the crow, now small
and dislocated:

a charcoal smut against an open sky.

Hatchling

Myanmar, the Hukawng Valley.
Never-to-become-skylark, hatched
to fly but drowned floundering in resin,
is held up to the light.
Feathers. Clawed foot. Beak.

X-rayed, carbon-dated, catalogued.
Cretaceous.
Ninety million years of soft tissue
and plumage to examine,
each filament brown as boiled sugar.

Wrong-footed by an unknown call,
slipping from the haphazard nest,
it tumbled to its death,
the last whirr of wingbeat, its claws,
catching only shadows.

From another planet, a distant universe,
we could watch it fall.
We could catch it, set it safely down,
watch it blinking, rebalancing its head
on that thin-string neck.

The light is amber.
Something caught, a moment unaware,
its wisp-legs broken,
strands of light its wings,
settles and stills.

Woman

It has the brilliance of fish, her skin,
mottled like oil on water.

We break her, pound her with stones,
beat flat the shards, beat them to a sharp edge,

beat them thinner until they slice leather,
pierce walrus hide or whale, cut bone.

We tell him she came from the stars,
crashed in plumes of steam.

He gives us knives and guns and wood,
packs up the bones of our dead,

promises gifts, and takes her,
sails her balanced on ice, to his ship.

She grows cold in the air, her pits and dents
messages cast by shadow.

We watch her leave, the sullen sea
tilting up to claim her.

Note: 'Woman' was one of the larger pieces of the Cape York Meteorite that
was used by Greenland Inuit for many centuries to create metal tools. It was
taken to New York by Robert Peary in 1897 where he sold it to the Museum
of Natural History.

Wild Horses
Lucie McKnight Hardy

The cigarettes had occurred to her somewhere over Greenland. The man in the adjacent seat had fallen asleep almost as soon as they'd taken off from Atlanta, and his head had lolled and then bounced onto her shoulder, causing her to shrink herself against the window. An hour later, something about the perfect pluming whiteness of the clouds and the sly reek of smoke twisting from her neighbour had conspired to induce in her a hankering for a smoke, even though she hadn't had one in twenty years. When they land at Heathrow, she told herself, she would go straight to the WHSmith in arrivals and buy a packet.

It must be something about going home. To Alison her hometown—for this is how she must still regard it—is a place of Marlboro Lights and Southern Comfort-and-lemonade; of pints of warm lager, and fish and chips eaten hot from the paper before the vinegar has a chance to evaporate, the wrapping chucked down the alley to decorate the sleeping drunks. It's a stagnant, stagnating place, a scene of abominations and yearnings, of skirts rucked around hips, the stone of the wall harsh against buttocks. Sodden thighs and monthly-bated-breath. And now she's going back.

Felix had dropped her at the short stay parking at the airport— 'It's a fortune to park here these days'—with a flaccid pat on the knee. 'Don't do anything I wouldn't do,' had been his final words, the manicured hand he'd wafted out of the window as he drove away betrayed by the swollen veins of late middle age. Both abandoned and emancipated, with two suitcases and an overnight bag, Alison made her way to check-in. The dislike she felt for her husband caused her to bristle, the once-blistering stream of loathing that had grown tepid through familiarity now scorching again.

*

She sits, one leg in, one leg out of the driver's side of the hire car, and scrapes at the cellophane with her thumbnail; it's rituals such as these that never die. She scrolls back the cardboard lid, and as though twenty years have suddenly been erased, her fingers know the exact dance to extract the foil from the top of the pack.

She slides a cigarette out with her thumb and lays it in her palm; it looks innocent enough. She sniffs the end, where tobacco sprouts, shrivelled and friable, and then she places it on her knee and picks up her bag from the passenger seat. Her new lipstick is in the inside pocket: Rimmel. She'd bought it at the airport, in the pharmacy in arrivals. They've changed all the names, of course, but she's found an approximation of the shade she used to wear. 'Alarm' it's called, a bright, bloody crimson. She pulls off the lid. After dragging down the sun visor and finding herself in the mirror, she runs the lipstick around her mouth, her lips instantly slick and moist and red. Its taste awakens a faint trace of memory, no more than a relic of her youth.

Her lips are sticky around the cigarette when it enters her mouth, and her hand trembles slightly with sleep deprivation and delicious anticipation as the lighter's flame soars. With the first inhalation she can taste the heat of the fire that engulfs the tobacco, that sears her lungs, but she tries again, and soon the familiar chemical thrill is threading its way through her veins. She grins and groans and leans back in the driver's seat. She's just taken ten years off herself and the old days seem tangible. Coming home isn't so hard.

*

The sat nav tells her three and a half hours, so she lines up an old Manics album on her phone and pairs it with the car's audio. She's nervous about driving on the left for the first time in so long, so she manoeuvres the hire car into the slip of a lorry in the slow lane and settles in. The drive along the M4 is uneventful and then, abruptly, the Severn Bridge appears, and she fumbles one-handed for her purse to pay the toll before she remembers that they've scrapped that now. When she first met Felix he'd made some joke about it being unfair that you had to pay to get into Wales—surely most people would pay to get out? He'd glanced around the other men who stood at the bar when he said that and grinned, waiting for laughter to be manufactured, his lazy anticipation that of the very wealthy who have grown accustomed to fawning subordinates. The other men hadn't even made eye contact with him; they heard this same joke all the time from the out-of-towners.

She stops at a service station to use the bathroom and buy something to drink. It's a mild afternoon but the sky is a blank grey canvas, just starting to darken. She leans against the side of the car and half smokes another cigarette, then grinds the last inch into the tarmac with her heel. Onwards.

It's the dismal beauty of Port Talbot that makes her feel as though she's on the cusp of a return. The heaving chimneys, silhouetted against an empty sky, chug out great white plumes: a salutation. After another half an hour or so, she comes off the motorway and approaches the town. Over the first roundabout and the road pitches and there are the electricity pylons. Four of them, skeletal and persistent against the now pinking sky. At school they used to say that if you stood under them for too long your brain would fry, and of course she and some of the others had tried it, camping out under the great scraggy megaliths, having strung together a story for their parents. No one's brain had fried but there is, nevertheless, something intransigent about them, a stolid, unchanging presence that unsettles.

She decides to drive in along the back road, avoiding the High Street for now, and follows signs to a new multi-storey car park. It seems it is part of a development where the old cattle market used to be, a shopping centre: Zara, L'Occitane, Gap. A brand new cinema, solidified in homogenous red brick, a last-ditch attempt to breathe life into this grey town. It's late afternoon now. Liver-hued and wet to the eye, the sky is pregnant with the threat of rain.

The Lonely Crowd - Issue Fourteen

Sleep has eluded her for more than twenty-four hours, and she feels that heady mix of jetlag-induced somnolence coupled with the confounding thump of Red Bull. She'd tried to sleep on the plane, of course, but the lolling man had added to his misdemeanours with staccato snoring, so it had been a fitful, prickled sleep. She'd dreamed little and often, bright flashes: vignettes that illuminated her brain for what seemed like seconds when she woke, but could have lasted any number of milliseconds or minutes. Footsteps on cobbles, the clatter of bottles and a brief flash of white, vulnerable flesh. She woke, parched, somewhere over the Atlantic, with the sensation of trying to clutch at water.

*

Since she had come to the realisation that she could leave Felix, she's always known she'd come back here, despite her attempts to kid herself that the world was her oyster. She pretended that she was genuinely considering renting a car to drive across the States, or that she might live in Europe for a bit and make the most of it before the effects of Brexit really kicked in and she'd need a visa. But the inevitability of a return to her hometown was insurmountable, a highway with no exits and nowhere to turn around, and so she invented a hitherto unmentioned and recently deceased aunt, booked her flight, and left.

She considers another smoke before she gets out of the car but can feel the dry ache in the back of her throat and thinks she will save them for later. She wonders if Sandra still smokes. A lot of people vape now instead but she doesn't think of Sandra as that sort. No, Sandra was always a slave to the cigarettes, lighting up as soon as she'd finished her shift. Alison smiles to think of her old boss: head thrown back, elbow propped, cigarette inserted between sphincter-like lips, taking that first hard drag on the other side of the bar. 'Jesus Christ, Ali, I need this,' as though she'd been working down a coal pit all day, rather than a six-hour shift in the Ceffyl Du.

127

Alison had been surprised to learn that Sandra was still there after all this time. Once she'd consolidated her thoughts about leaving Felix, the first thing she had done was to consider her options for going home. She couldn't face trying to contact any of the school friends she'd lost touch with, could already anticipate their stifled glee when she would have to admit that it hadn't worked out in America. Her parents couldn't help—they had died within months of each other six years ago. She'd wanted to come back for the funeral, of course, but they'd never been that close, and in the end Felix had persuaded her that she'd only find it distressing. They hadn't included her in their wills. It was when Alison was considering her employment prospects that she'd thought about Sandra and tracked her down on Facebook. If she was going back home, she'd need a job, and she was hardly qualified to do much these days, was she? Their correspondence had been sparse, almost stilted, but Sandra had agreed that there were a few shifts she could pick up and had even said she could stay in one of the pub's empty rooms upstairs.

In the rear-view mirror, Alison reapplies her lipstick and then takes the smaller of her two suitcases from the trunk—she'll have to get used to saying boot again—and locks the car. It's a ten minute walk to the Ceff, and she plots her route using her memories of pub crawls of the past. They'd start off at the Coracle on East Street and then head up Drover's Alley for a swift one in the Fleece, before grappling with the sticky doors and floors of the Angel and its crowds of young men, greedy with lust, their faces lupine, keen. The girls had relished the attention, had enjoyed the hunger evident in the opposition's eyes, and they'd accept the offers of drinks and cigarettes and then pile out onto the pavement a squawking, tumbling mass, and saunter on to the next place.

It won't be long before the shops start to empty, and the pubs fill up. It's a Saturday, so she'll need to get to the pub before the place gets too crowded; it used to get packed to the rafters after a match. It was on one of those Saturdays, when she'd been nearing the end of her shift, that Felix had elbowed his way up to the bar. He wasn't much to look at: pale, slight, thinning on top, and a good twenty years older than her. Not someone she would have normally noticed or wasted any attention on, but when he'd leant over the bar and asked for a neat Scotch, she'd immediately caught the lazy drone of his accent, which carried with it a hint of the exotic, a faint transatlantic promise of something new. When her shift finished, he'd bought her a drink, and they'd chatted a bit. She enjoyed his fascination with her body, how his gaze was drawn to her skin where it was revealed by the sparse fabric of her top. It was a familiar feeling, the power bestowed by flesh, the sheer desire the meat of her could instil in a man. It made her feel perversely unassailable, as though she was in possession of something priceless, an asset which made her capable of negotiation. When he suggested they go and sit in his car, she'd half-heartedly wondered if he was going to try to screw her. He did, and she let him, and she had looked on, disinterested, as her body made all the right signs of enjoyment. Afterwards, she'd wiped herself down and given him directions to the coast.

She'd always felt at peace there: a ten minute drive from town, it was a barren and windswept place, backed by sand dunes and with a long flat shoreline and a view to the other side of the estuary that was occasionally dotted with sailing dinghies and the odd fishing boat. Sometimes, there were wild horses that wandered in from the grassy lowlands, and they would run with abandon, hooves kicking up the sand, their eyes wild. There, he'd parked the car and, because there hadn't been anyone around, she'd let him lean her over the bonnet of the car and fuck her again.

Afterwards, he'd suggested she might go and stay with him for a while. Nothing heavy, just visit for a couple of weeks, have a look around the area. If she liked it, she could stay longer. It would be a chance to get out of this shithole. When he said that she'd felt an odd stirring of loyalty for her town, for where she'd grown up, which had quickly dissipated: the last dregs of bathwater swirling down the plug hole.

Two weeks later she was on a plane. He'd sent her the money for the flight—business class. She'd given Sandra a week's notice and while the older woman had rolled her eyes and sucked away on her cigarette, you could tell that she was envious of Alison's pending liberation.

It was Sandra who'd suggested the lock-in on Alison's last night—just the regulars, plus half a dozen rugby-types who were over from Llanelli and hadn't been causing any trouble. Sandra had been drinking since early evening, her smile getting loose and slick, her plum lipstick smearing jammily around her mouth. Tactile, and with an extra button undone on her blouse, she flitted between customers, her smattering laughter too loud. She'd taken the piss out of the Llanelli boys, calling them 'bufty boys in your chinos and Ben Sherman shirts,' which got a laugh from the locals, but hard stares from the rugby players. There was one in particular, a small, whippy guy who would probably have played on the wing, who held Alison's eye for a long moment, longer than was necessary, before looking back into his pint glass. Later, he'd tried to feel her up on her way back from the bathroom, had pushed her up against the wall, his face too close to hers, reeking of beer and testosterone. She'd shoved him away and gone to stand behind the bar.

*

Dragging her suitcase along behind her, Alison wonders what she will tell Sandra about her twenty-year adventure that had started off with so much promise: a life with a millionaire restaurant owner that had turned into marriage (pre-nup, of course) before the indifference crystallised into mutual dislike and then a sharp loathing, merely a year or two later.

At first, her life had consisted of the gym and shopping trips, paid for by Felix, and meals out (at his own restaurants) and lots of sex, the likes of which she hadn't encountered in her brief history of Tesco's car park and the bus station. Felix's tastes were wide-ranging and relentless, and even though she agreed to stay on after the initial two-week holiday, she found herself increasingly perturbed by his predilections. The persistence of the rumours about Felix's dalliances with the younger waiting staff was a constant low-frequency buzz in her self-esteem, an insect that would hover, unseen, its drone a mild but relentless irritant.

After a while, she stopped going to the gym, and instead spent her time at coffee shops and bakeries, ordering more than she could possibly eat and cramming the sweet distractions into her mouth with expensively manicured fingers. As an anticipated result, her youthful angularity gave way to softer, more pliable curves, and Felix took to spending longer at his restaurants, where his employees had the jutting hip bones of teenagers and the wholesome tooth-whitened zest of catalogue models.

*

When the tarmacked pavement gives way to cobbles, the suitcase bumps painfully along behind her. The chip shop on Church Street is just opening, the first oleaginous guffs pumping through the open door. A group of teenaged girls is tottering foal-like on too-high heels on the corner, their shoulders poking, goose-pimpled and vulnerable, from strappy tops. She wasn't that much older than them when she left this town and she hopes they have better luck than she did. Turning left at the bingo hall, she pushes the button at the pedestrian crossing. A car approaches from behind, and there's a shout: 'Alright, love?' Instinctively, she straightens: belly in, tits out. The car passes, and she sees young men—boys, really—hanging out of the back windows. 'Sorry, grandma,' comes the cry, and there's a collective guffaw as the car disappears around the corner. The skin on the back of her hand feels papery dry against her mouth as she swipes away the lipstick.

Finally, she is standing at the bottom of the High Street, looking up the faint incline, and she can just about make out the sign that hangs perpendicular to the wall of the pub. A black horse, rearing up on its hind legs, the paint flaking now and faded.

*

It was only when the true nature of the revelations about Felix's behaviour were made known that she started to entertain the notion that she could leave him. For years they'd plodded on, their marriage silently acknowledged to be a mistake, but neither of them with the energy or inclination to do anything about it. They each knew about the others' indiscretions, and even if his were more transgressive than hers, she let him get away with it, because what was the point of rocking the boat? She finds it difficult to pinpoint the exact moment it had dawned on her that she could leave. It wasn't a lightbulb moment, more a gradual enlightenment, a glacial shifting of a realisation that she didn't have to stay—there was nothing tying her to their house and the restaurants. It really was as easy as packing her bags and going home.

*

Sandra is behind the bar and she doesn't look up. She's pouring a pint for an old guy who's perched on one of the bar stools, the usual sort: flat cap, tweed jacket that will be pungently reminiscent of sheep dip and creosote. Sandra's hair is still bleached and scraggy, and pulled up in a tight ponytail on the top of her head—what they'd have called a council facelift, back in the day. She's scrawny-thin, but the tops of her arms where they peer from the sleeves of her blouse are glutinous, like cheap ice cream melting in the tub. She's still wearing the low-cut tops, and Alison can see the curve of her breasts, hoisted artificially high, wrinkled and parched. When Sandra does look up, Alison is absurdly shocked that she is still wearing her trademark plum lipstick. At her age.

At first, neither woman says anything, and silence sits between them, as thick and stultifying as tide-sodden sand. Then Sandra lifts the flap at the end of the bar and walks very deliberately towards Alison, her careful gait alluding to the fact that she will have been on the Malibu since the start of her shift, unless something's changed.

'Well. Look at you then.' Alison feels stripped bare, vulnerable, as Sandra's eyes travel over her body; there is no trace of the potency she would feel as a young woman when men and boys would appraise her form. Sandra's gaze is critical, assessing. 'We've neither of us got any younger, have we?' the older woman barks, and a flame of indignation sparks in Alison's chest. Sandra must be, what? Ten, fifteen years older than her? She is suddenly conscious of the added weight around her hips, the fat that creases her belly.

'You still on the cancer sticks, then Sandra? Not good for the complexion, you know.' It's cruel, and she's sorry as soon as she's said it, but Sandra doesn't seem to mind.

'Yeah. I was just going out the back for one, matter of fact, before it starts to fill up in here. You coming?'

Alison feels as though she's been wrongfooted, as though her need to defend herself by taking down the other woman has cast her as the villain. Still, she tells herself, they must be allies if this new life of hers is going to work. She starts to tell Sandra that she doesn't smoke anymore, then remembers the packet of Marlboro Lights in her handbag. 'Any chance of a drink with that?'

Sandra gives her a wink and retreats behind the bar. She doesn't ask what Alison wants, but instead pours a double measure of Southern Comfort into a glass and tops it up with a splash of lemonade from the tap. No ice. She looks pleased with herself.

'See? Twenty years and I haven't forgotten.' She picks up a half pint of brown liquid from under the bar which Alison knows will contain as much Malibu as it does Coke, and leads the way through the outside door that will take them into the alley.

It hasn't changed. None of it. The same whitewashed brick wall, the crates of empty bottles, the damp air that is lit now by the pale orange streetlight. Alison will wonder later if it is these prompts which summon the memory. That last night at the pub, and her sudden realisation that Sandra wasn't in the bar and that Alison was doing all the serving. Going to look for her—first in the ladies' and then outside in the alley. Sandra, pushed up against the wall by the rugby player from Llanelli, blouse ripped open, bra torn. Breasts bare, eyes wide, feral. Pleading. The bottle in Alison's hand, grabbed from one of the empty crates, and smashing down on the side of the man's head, the resulting crack shockingly satisfying in the silence of the alley. His hand up at his temple and Sandra wriggling free and Alison raising the bottle again. And he'd bolted. Just like that, he ran away, disappeared down the alley. At that moment, Alison had felt a power unlike any other. Then the soothing, the smoothing of clothes, the drying of tears, the embrace.

Alison has no recollection of what came after. Her next memory is of boarding the flight at Heathrow the following morning, her excitement tempered only slightly by her hangover.

*

'Got a light?' Sandra asks, wriggling out a cigarette and placing it between her lips. Alison juggles her drink and fishes in her bag, and finally retrieves the lighter. She flicks it and leans forward, Sandra's free hand cupping around it to shield it from the breeze.

'Jesus Christ, Ali, I need this,' says Sandra after blowing out a stream of smoke. The two women lean against the whitewashed wall, sucking and puffing and sipping in silence.

Of the past, they do not speak. It is there, in the broken glass glittering in the amber glow of the streetlight; in the yeasty bloom rising from the crates of empty beer bottles and in the silence that inhabits the space between them. A brittle, friable silence, that could crumble at any moment.

It is there in the flutter of fingers against the back of Alison's hand.

'Welcome home, girl. Welcome home.'

Three Poems
Jo Mazelis

A Fairy Story

Nothing so white as the reindeer's flank
on which the child has rested.
This is the real world, or is it?
Once, on Harlech Crescent, in the room,
in the bed where my great grandmother
had dwelt, I read the Snow Queen.
In the garden, a Christmas tree that someone,
some January, had planted after the war,
a gooseberry bush (the one they found my sister under)
and a ruby-red peony with a drumstick head
big as his fist. Ice and whiteness,
hot pennies pressed against glass,
Kay going off (how could he?) like a gullible fool.

Gerda, so steadfast, going after,
in a boat on a stream, to meet along
the way, the little robber girl. Here she lies now.
Ruddy-cheeked, fast asleep.
Nothing so warm as the reindeer's flank
or my great grandmother's bed,
her eiderdown full of dreams and feathers.
A story ending on a skein of wool, a skein of geese.

A Woman Demented by Dust

She clawed, cat-like up the window,
saying she must clean, but only spreading smears.
Splashes from her dampened rag fell on the people
at the dinner party beneath
and a tall man – her son or son-in-law
tried to prise her from the wall

or waited to catch her, should she fall.
A small child wailed in the corridor,
woken by the commotion,
beside herself with weeping.

Everyone exhausted.
As much from pretence
as sorely tried patience.
The girl's mother rolled her eyes
as the child wailed on,
helpless, not understanding
what was wrong.

'I think I know what it is,' I said
and like a saviour, rose
from my harp-backed, rosewood
chair, the table of glittering crystal,
the immaculate setting and silver
soldiers of forks and knives
who lay on their backs,
waiting for slaughter
on the field of starched white linen,
and left them for my mission.

Rising and Falling Like the Tide

Always in dreams a staircase rising,
lifting its tide of feet, the stone spiral pristine
and when the time came, they lifted her head
from its basket of straw and wrapped it tenderly.
No man should touch her body despite the balm,
when living, she poured into theirs.
This is what we do to preserve our children,
lie and flatter, soothe and smother darker truths.
What is ugly must be hidden, wrapped in fine lawn linen.
Her blood (imagine how much there must have been;
the neck struck clean, the sparrow heart fluttering
and rushing to stem the tide) and
for the others, those men accused;
one a musician, they were already by then,
just notes like larks ascending,
or footfalls distantly descending.

The Bangle
Angela Graham

I walk to work. I sometimes come to the cemetery on the way. From there I can look down on the whole town, and the sea, below me. I have a word with Mam. There's never much to tell her, usually. But she likes to hear how I'm getting on.

I'm glad she died just before the pandemic. It was bad enough without that. But she died well. She was brave. The nurses said that. She made an effort for them, I think, because they were coming to her home and she wanted them to feel welcome. She'd tell them she worried about me. About what I'd do in the future. I used to say *Maybe I'll be a nurse.* And she liked that. A career. She worried because when I should have been thinking of my future she got ill and there were only the two of us. So it was obvious. I took care of her. But when she died, lockdown happened and I wasn't going anywhere then, was I?

Yeah, from the cemetery you can see the whole town; people moving about; traffic. Growing up here you think it's normal that its population ebbs and flows. Holiday-makers in and out; students next. The prom heaving with people; the prom empty; the big university buildings like white cliffs behind the Victorian boarding-houses on the front. I don't think us locals get noticed, really. We take money in the shops; wait tables; bake bread; make beds...

That day I had the 5pm shift at the Home, which I like, because after tea the residents have bedtime on their minds so there aren't so many crises. I've been there since the first lockdown. I knew about caring and they were desperate to have anyone who would live in. What else had I to do? And I knew about dying. There was a lot of that. The pandemic's behind us now but I haven't moved on.

The Home's on the prom. It's a couple of those tall, old houses knocked together. All along the sea-front, terraces of buildings just like it peer at the sea, day and night, from lots of windows. Walking towards the Home I was thinking how you can feel the house resisting the sea. In front of them there's one barrier after another against the waves: pavement, tarmac, promenade, iron railings, stone bulwark and finally a steep breakwater. All to keep the sea in its place. No wonder it gets irritable. It sort of loiters about, being wet. It can't muster the energy to leap up over the prom. It's got the habits of a sea – tides, waves, foam – but not the oompf.

So the eruption of a man from the terraces was – a shock. Darting through the slow parade of cars, sprinting across the prom and vaulting the railings, he dropped onto the shingle, landed in a neat crouch, righted himself and sprang forward, dashing towards the sea. Chasing what? A figure, struggling against the colourless water. Someone with long, white hair and white clothes. After a few strides the man floundered, then launched himself in a rugby tackle, disappearing briefly. Up he came, and then turned back to the shore, with the white figure in his arms. I ran down the steps to the beach and he came towards me like a groom carrying his bride. Her trailing hair, her nightdress, poured sea-water. Her face was white; her limbs, frail.

'Mrs Bailey!' I cried, amazed. 'Ambulance,' he gasped.

'Too slow. She's from the Home.' I sent him up the steps with his burden. Some staff were waiting to shepherd him away. And then I saw something gold glinting in the shingle. A bangle. Its outer face was worn and scratched but the inside was smooth, like new. There were words inscribed there in a lovely, flowing script: *'To Frances. Forever From Now On – George'*. It must have slipped from Mrs Bailey's wrist.

She hadn't been in the Home long. She'd come from another town, along with a reputation for being difficult. I'd found her easy enough, though too quiet. Depressed, probably. She was well into her nineties but she could get about. Her mind was sharp. She liked to see a newspaper. She'd notice the difference between a thing done well and a thing done badly and tell you. She didn't always want to get dressed and you'd find she'd made her way, in her nightie, to the nook on the front landing that was a vantage point for the whole Bay. The home couldn't let her sit there, *undressed*, as Melanie put it. There would be (there were) complaints. She was stubborn more than difficult, I'd say, and mostly just unhappy. She never said why it was important to her to look out like that.

When I reached the Home there was a fuss, of course. *How had she got out? Who'd left the door unlocked? What if she'd got knocked down?* Melanie, the Senior on duty at the time, was terrified the news would get out. She was saying to the man, 'We take great care of our residents, Mr...?'

'Cairns. Ian.'

'This has never happened before. If you hadn't come along....'

He was dripping onto the tiled floor of the hallway. In a suit. 'Mr Cairns needs some dry clothes,' I said. Melanie's eyes were on the residents who were gawping from the banisters overhead and crowding the doorways of the Lounge. 'I'll take him to the Laundry and see what I can find, shall I?' A nod from her and she was off, shooing them away. I took the man out the back. He was in his thirties, lightly built but fit. I found him some things. I couldn't help smiling when he re-appeared, zipping up a hideous green cardigan.

'I look like my granda,' he grinned. I held up a pair of open-toed sandals. 'To complete the outfit?' he asked. As he put them on, he said, 'I've just come from a job interview. Glad I wasn't on my way *to* it.' He straightened up. 'Why did she do it?'

'I don't know. At least.... Well, she does sit and look at the sea for ages at a time. Maybe she just decided to make a break for it.'

He thought about this. He shook his head. 'She opened her eyes and smiled at me. She said, 'edge', or 'judge', or something, but then she realised she didn't know me after all and passed out.'

Then Melanie rushed up and carried him away into the Office. He looked back just before she closed the door and I waved to him before I had time to think that was an odd thing to do to someone I didn't know.

Poor Mrs Bailey got the Third Degree next day. *What were you thinking of? Don't you realise...?* And so on. Category A prisoner she'd be from now on. She needs watching, that one,' Melanie said to me.

'She must have had it thought through beforehand – how to get out.' Mrs Bailey just turned that bangle and looked past Melanie, as though she was expecting someone to come to the door. I'd noticed that since *her episode*, as Melanie kept calling it, she'd taken to pulling the bangle off and putting it back on with a gesture that was like locking a manacle in place. The bangle had one of those old-fashioned clasps that opened it on a hinge and there was a delicate little chain supposed to keep the halves from opening too wide. And she still insisted on getting to that vantage-point.

Several days later Ian Cairns turned up, to see how she was getting on, he said. I brought them tea and left them talking by that big window. And she certainly did talk to him. I watched him, bending towards her, nodding. He came back the week after too, and the next, and I wished I had someone who'd listen to me like that. He had a lovely smile.

One morning, early, I saw him jogging down the prom but he'd gone past before I could wave. I watched for him but I didn't see him again on his own like that.

It was almost as though Melanie knew I looked forward to his visits because she kept me in the Laundry or out the back as soon as he appeared. I think she had her eye on him for herself. Some of the other girls certainly did. He was so full of energy, though he moved quietly. We weren't used to energy in the Home. The girls went on about, *Why is he paying Mrs B so much attention? Is he after her money? Has she got any?*

After more than a month I was coming from the Laundry with a pile of sheets as he was leaving. He came over to me and said, 'I got that job. I started last week. Phlebotomist in the surgery. I've been wondering where you were.'

'Still here,' I said. I heard myself sounding hopeless.

'Mrs Bailey likes you.'

'She does?'

'Yes. You gave her the bangle back.'

'I didn't think she notice.'

'She sees a lot.' He smiled at me. And then he asked me to meet him when I finished my shift. I nearly fell over. I think I carried those sheets upstairs in a daze.

We sat in a café on the prom and he told me… all about Mrs Bailey.

Mrs Bailey, he said, had been a widow for years. When she was young, she had fallen in love with a man her family disapproved of. A Jew. 'In Nineteen-forty-four she was nineteen and he was in the army. They'd sworn secretly to marry after the war but he didn't come back. She waited and waited. Nothing. An older man paid her a lot of attention. He was rich and influential. All she had to do was say yes and the whole family would benefit. She resisted for a year. Then another. No word from….'

'George! But he must have come back because the bangle says….'

'Well, he did come back. But her mother answered the door. And she let him have it. What did he think he was doing, turning up out of the blue like this? Frances was about to be engaged to a very nice man so he should clear off and leave her to be happy. That's what he would do if he really loved her. She didn't call Frances to the door till she'd had her say. But, of course, it wasn't the happy reunion Frances had longed for. He was awkward and hesitant. He was holding a little package. Was that for her? 'I'm not sure,' he said, you know, miserably. He held it out to her and she took it but she was so disappointed she got angry. When he asked her, probing, like, and still on the doorstep, whether she'd been seeing anyone else while he'd been away, she said, 'Maybe I have. I've certainly had plenty of time to!' and left him there. She was so sure of him, in her heart. She thought it would be just a moment, really….'

'But she didn't know what her mother had said.' I could see her – petulant, afraid. 'Still, he'd left the bangle.'

Ian nodded. 'He had it made in the Far East where he'd been stationed. And then he'd got ill, and then kind of marooned. He'd meant it as a way of showing her they'd be together….'

'Forever From Now On.'

She was sure he'd come back. But he re-enlisted. Gone within days.'

'And she married Mr Bailey.'

I thought of her. Sitting by that window in the Home, looking out.

'She's still waiting. Is she?'

We both went silent. And something made us both look at the sea. You could count your life out in waves, I thought, one by one.

Ian sighed. 'Well, something happened, recently. She saw something in the paper. George's funeral notice. He died here – in the town.'

So close, and not knowing! 'He never married.'

I was speechless.

Ian went on. 'She said, 'He left me because he loved me. He stayed away because he loved me.' It overwhelmed her – all over again. As though it'd happened last week. She said that coming to the Home – her 'last home', she said – made her look back across her whole life and all its choices. She couldn't fathom how she'd let her life be steered – that's how she put it – by vanity and pride and how she hadn't gone after what really mattered; she'd expected it to come to her. She should have gone looking for George. And now it was too late. So she watched the sea. 'It just arrives', she said. 'It's got no imagination. Same time every day. Come in. Go out. That's where I should be, in that mediocre sea.''

'And you pulled her out.' And why are you telling me all this, I wondered.

As though he'd heard me, he said, 'So. I need your help, to get her out of the Home.'

'Out of…!'

'Without anyone knowing,' he insisted. *'Kidnapping* her?'

'Only for a couple of hours. No, I mean, look, she wants to go to his grave, but *discreetly*. I can't manage alone.' I hesitated. It wasn't a great job I had at the Home but still… 'She wants to put the bangle into the earth, before the grave is re-settled.'

Mrs Bailey. Regret. Remorse. For a lost chance with George. For all, for anything, she ought to have done and hadn't; for the love she could have had and threw away. Frances and George. 'OK,' I said.

Then I looked at Ian Cairns for a long time. I asked Mrs Bailey for some courage. And I said to him, 'I like you.'

Forever From Now On has to start somewhere.

Two Poems
Fiona Cameron

Speculum Alchimiae

Barnacre, Year Unknown

It is not 1588

> It is 1988

We are not peasant children

> We do not have a dog

We do not have shell suits

> But we do have rah rah skirts

We are playing in the far fields

> We use dried out cow pats as frisbees

We have been told not to do this

> We have also been told not to play near the deep pond

We have ignored this

> We do not have a dog

We have played here all afternoon

> We watch the weeping willows that disturb the surface tension

We hear the slow wind that troubles their leaves

> We like the reddish clay we gather on the steep banks

We fashion it into pots in the old cow shed

> We are running a cottage industry

We love its thick rich feeling

> We love its earthy smell

We love our impressive wares

> We are filthy

We are bone cold

> We do not have a dog

We watch the winter sun setting

                            We see winding field mist rising

We cannot see the house from back here

                    We cannot see the lights from the kitchen

We cannot hear any voices but our own

                          And the air is prickling now

We do not have a dog

*

It is not 1588

            Is it not?

                      There is a dog

                              It is not a poodle

It is not a shih tzu

                        It is not a bouncing collie

It is dark and shifting

      It is a medieval zig zag

            It huffs from its pointed face

                  It is formed of grey shaggy fur

          It has walked in lopsided   as if from a tapestry

          A skinny haunch – arched and precision sprung

                      It has loosed stitches

                somewhere in the reverse of now

                  It tilts time across the back and sides of

        the field

      It paws unpredictable circles inward

It has crossed an invisible line

                  It has arrived from nowhere

We do not want a dog

It is not 1588
It is 1988

Is it not a dog?

On the fish scale

time is measured in annuli.
Circular regions, denotative of
a lifespan spent below.

In this medieval fishpond,
a fish scale is all you need to
confirm these silver gilled slabs have
always moved sinuous
beneath you
sculling up water
against your airy human tenure.

The circular region of the mouth,
is as blank as the moon.
Breaks the meniscus, opening upwards to
receive an insect on the microscopic scale.
The flash of milliseconds.

Or lifetimes.

The mayfly hovers tentative, halts, moves on
and into the dying scale of the summer night.
The monks of Birkenhead Priory and nuns of
Chester have long since relinquished these
ponds,
they need them no more,
but the fish scale continues to evolve, to move
deep. It repeats in circles and disturbs marl
in swirls at the turning of the centuries.

Hurry along now won't you.

Lingering here as your low sun sets,
will surely just return you to the start.

Take Away
Alan McCormick

Visiting day, the curtains have been opened, the untouched takeaway removed, and the evil commode wheeled from my room.

Mum is talking in the hall: you'll have to be quieter today. She's struggling and noise is really bothering her but seeing you will cheer her up. Go on now, she won't bite.

Yasmine and Sarah come into my room.

Heh, Hannah, look what we've got you!

A huge card. I raise my head off the pillows. Three Labrador puppies on the cover.

They open it up: Ta-da!

Wince.

Sorry, too loud? Everyone's signed it this time. Even Michelle Mayes.

Grimace.

They laugh.

Bubble writing, kisses, love hearts, smileys. Too much. I can't keep my head up anymore. Back I go. Eyes shut. Tight as I can.

We'll read it for you.

Taking turns. Yasmine first: Laura says *hang in there, babes, we all love you*.

And Jane says *we missssssss you*. One, two, three . . .that's seven s's.

She must really miss you! says Yasmine.

Gemma says *you're the best and I hate what's happening to you*, continues Sarah.

That makes me want to cry.

But when I open my eyes, it's Yasmine who's crying.

I rest my palm on her cheek.

Don't, Yas, it's all right.

No, it isn't, she says, kissing me, holding me close.

Sarah stares at us. She looks sad and unsure what to do, so she reads on: Mrs Fox says *I loved teaching you* . . .

Swot! Yasmine whispers in my ear.

And can't wait to teach you again. Keep strong and we'll undoubtedly see you soon. Shall I carry on?

I shake my head and mouth thank you.

Undoubtedly: what a stupid word, says Yasmine.

Can we do anything for you? asks Sarah.

I shake my head and close my eyes again.

They find a way to get into my bed. One lying on either side. We hold hands and I don't want to let go. I like their heat. The smell of their sunny outside skin. As I feel myself go under, I hear Yasmine singing – *sail here, let me hold you* – and when I surface, they're gone.

I press the buzzer and Mum rushes in like a dog is chasing her.

Weeks later, and Robert Smith is singing 'Close to Me' on the cassette player by my bed. I've always loved that song but today it hurts; everything from tip to toe tingling, aching, as if my body is riddled with some ancient plague coursing poison through my veins. I slide myself off the bed and onto the commode. A sick geriatric trickle when I'm fifteen, and in my prime apparently. I must have been an evil witch in my previous life!

Only those kinds of thoughts are supposed to be banned from my psyche since Katherine the counsellor has been visiting me:

Keep in the moment, no blaming, and look forward rather than back without putting any pressure on yourself, tiny steps at a time.

She doesn't know about the stumbling witch-like steps to hell, might save that for another session.

The witchy nightmare started over a year ago when I was diagnosed with glandular fever. I was off school for six weeks. When I returned, I was greeted with a mixture of envy and sympathy, and perhaps – though I may have been exaggerating it in my head – suspicion.

Envy came from glandular fever's reputation as the kissing disease.

So, who have you been snogging?

Did you go further?

Bet she did.

Was it worth it to get ill?

Yasmine stepped in: She was kissing me, and it's none of your business if we went further. And, of course, it was worth it, eh, Hannah?

Suspicion came from me looking too well for someone who was off school for so long.

My brother had glandular fever and he was only off for a week!

He didn't have glandular fever then, said Yasmine.

Maybe you were kissing him, Hannah, said Michelle Mayes.

Some of the girls – not all – laughed.

Anyway, suspicion was something I'd need to get used to, as a month later I felt even worse and was diagnosed with M.E.

A few friends have stayed loyal, but it's hard when the Daily Mail keeps labelling M.E. *'yuppie flu'*, a *'malingerer's disease'* reserved for *'spoilt middle-class hypochondriacs.'*

My new loveable trait is to wake with pools of dribble on my pillowcase, a kind of paralysis of my tongue and bottom lip, as if I've had a minor stroke, so now when I speak, I'm like a drunk, gurning, slurring my words.

It's inexplicable, not mentioned in any textbook, not visible in any test but it is happening – at least I think it is – this illness can play tricks with you. There's so much disbelief that even I'm beginning to question what's real and what isn't.

The pillowcase is wet. Maybe I emptied my glass onto it in the night?

No, my glass is full. I'm *a glass full* kind of girl, surely.

As my symptoms worsen, Mum and Dad become desperate. They take me to A&E.

A doctor examines me. Makes me stand until my legs start to buckle. Then he drops his pen and asks me to pick it up from the floor. I say I'll fall if I do.

No, you won't, he says.

And like a good dog at Crufts, I perform the trick on all fours and hand it up to him.

Now I'd like you to get up too.

I can't.

I'm waiting.

Dad goes to help me.

Stay!

Good dog Dad does as he's told.

I've got all day, so take your time.

I think it's hatred that makes me somehow force myself off the floor.

Hey presto, he says.

I'm shaking and want to cry, but not in front of him.

You're being a prick! Dad tells him.

Wow, that makes me proud.

Maybe so. But I'm asking myself if you really want your daughter to be well? Maybe you should be asking yourselves that too?

Is that it? says Mum. You're not going to do anything for her?

M.E. is not a recognised illness, there's nothing physically wrong with her. Now, if you want me to call someone from the adolescent psych team to come down, I'd be more than happy to do that.

Come on, Hannah, says Dad, helping me on with my coat and into my wheelchair.

She doesn't need the chair either. I'll be recommending a follow up from social services in my report, just so you know.

Dad pushes the chair quickly away, a back wheel bouncing over the doctor's shoes as we leave.

Loving faces congregate around my open coffin. The wake has started. Crap music like a dirge is playing but the dancing is manic. Robert Smith is standing to the side like an exotic wallflower with his big hair, blood red lipstick and heavy clown mascara. He leans over my cask and uses his ring finger – a twisting coral viper – to smudge black eye shadow onto my eyelids. His breath is patchouli and Bovril crisps and when we kiss, I think I'm in heaven. Then the front doorbell rings, and seconds later Dad is knocking on my door.

Sorry, Hannah, the Assessment Team are here.

I thought they were coming next Wednesday.

I hear him tell them: you'll have to wait while she gets herself ready.

A woman's voice: Hannah can get herself ready then? Dress herself?

I don't know if she's getting dressed. I didn't say that. She just needs some time.

A man's voice – two of them then? Or maybe more? An army? – It's okay, we're here to help, not catch anyone out.

Sarah visits without Yasmine later in the day. I don't mention the assessment and tell her instead about my Robert Smith dream.

I like him too, she says, and then pauses. I can tell she's not sure whether to continue: Adam *(that's her brother)* says that girls who like Robert Smith don't really like boys at all. It's a sign.

Of what?

I'm only saying what Adam says.

Okay, so ask your Nazi brother Adam if he'd be happier if I fancied Frank Bruno?

Hannah, stop, I wish I hadn't said anything.

Me too.

Shall I go?

If you want to.

I'd rather stay.

Okay, I'd rather you stay, too.

Okay?

Okay!

We don't speak for a bit. Then I break the silence.

Have you seen Yasmine?

None of us has seen her in ages.

She can get reclusive sometimes.

She hasn't told you, has she?

Told me what?

That's she's been seeing someone.

No, she did!

Okay, I thought maybe –

She's told me all about her.

Hannah, she hasn't told you, it's not a 'her'; she's seeing a boy from another school. They met at a party. He's called Spike.

Ouch!

Hannah, come on.

The name is funny, that's all. She ought to watch where she sits.

Hannah, it's okay to be upset.

I'm not upset and stop saying my name: Hannah, Hannah? Hannah!

I know you.

You know my name.

Hannah, please.

You should go, *Sarah*.

I close my eyes and feign a coma, and eventually she gets the message.

At the door before she leaves, she says, I know you're not actually sleeping.

Yes, I am, I say quietly enough so even I can barely hear.

That day wiped me out for weeks and I disappeared into a fug – 'brain fog' which the M.E. handbook describes just doesn't cut it – a dirty toxic pea-soup fug. I slept, dribbled, and dreamt I was lying on my back, unable to move off a cold ocean bed, life shimmering above the surface of the water. Yasmine kept ringing, and I pretended to be asleep each time there was a knock on my door to ask if I was well enough to speak to her.

Eventually I tell Mum: Inform Yasmine that my fever's spiked. That I feel like I've been spiked.

Spiked?

Mum, repeat back to me what I said to you.

'You've been spiked, that your fever's spiked.' It's an odd way of describing it, that's all.

Mum, that's what I want you to say!

She goes off to relay the message and comes back a minute later.

Well, I told her exactly like you asked me to. And she said, 'tell her the spike will soon be over'. I'm not sure what's going on but is there something you're not telling me? Are you and Yasmine okay?

Never better.

And I disappear again, this time feeling a trickle of warmth seeping onto the ocean bed.

I hear Mum on the surface above, edgy and desperate: Hannah, please let's try a takeaway tonight, we all need cheering up!

A letter arrives the next day. Mum and Dad open my curtains a crack and sit on the end of my bed to share its contents. Mum starts:

Hannah, they're recommending an exercise programme; gradual exercises building up over time. They also want you to take a higher dose of the anti-depressants.

The ones I stopped taking because they were turning me into a zombie?

Dad continues and Mum takes my hand – teamwork – we're on your side, love.

Then Mum takes on the baton: Hannah, we know the anti-depressants didn't agree with you and that exercise could make you worse.

I feel a 'but' coming on.

Well, yes, they're worried that you're becoming underweight. We explained that you need to be on a low sugar, toxin free diet and that you find it hard to eat big meals, but –

I told you a 'but' was coming.

I'm afraid there are a few 'buts', love, says Dad.

Mum takes a deep breath: they want you to stop the painkillers.

No, no, they can't make me!

Maybe we could cut the dose a little? she suggests.

Ok, God, you're with them!

Hannah, I'm not but we have to try something. If they won't prescribe any more, they'd last twice as long if we cut them in half.

Get out of my room!

Hannah!

I summon all my energy and scream.

Dad tries to hug me, and I scream louder.

Come on, he says to Mum and takes her by the crook of the arm and leads her away.

We love you, Hannah, and we'll check on you later, he says at my door.

Mum returns a moment later, pulls the curtains closed and legs it out of the room.

I consider my options, evaluating the impact of reducing the painkillers first: the DFF118's that have helped when nothing else has. If they make me give them up, then I might as well be dead.

Mum and Dad have left their letter, by mistake (I think), on my bed.

We are concerned for the welfare of your daughter, Hannah, and are seeking to work together with all the family to ensure her wellbeing. Your signed agreement for the rehabilitation programme as outlined will ensure clarity regarding expectations – expectations? – *In rare cases, if a minor's* – so, that's what I am – *condition is deemed to have significantly worsened, and they are assessed to be in danger, either from themselves* – grammar! – *or as a result of actions by legal guardians entrusted with their care; or in situations where a contract is broken, where support and co-operation is not forthcoming for any prescribed programme* – yawn! – *steps may be legally taken to remove the minor* – from the mine? – *and place them under the care of the local authority* – Nazis!

I know it's not going to go well but I call Mum and Dad back and tell them that I'll start reducing the painkillers tomorrow. But I won't take the anti-depressants again, let alone increase the dose. As I see it, I'm not really depressed for any other reason than my life is extremely depressing, but I may start to jiggle my toes – one at a time – if it'll help.

I may even consider the threatened takeaways if they'll add a few pounds and help keep me home.

Things have become diabolical. Mum and Dad have started leaving me a half dose of the painkillers – less than a third of a bottle left – by my bed each morning. We're nervous, listening for the phone and doorbell, waiting for the authorities to take their next step.

Hope it doesn't end up like Waco, Dad.

That's not funny, Hannah.

But I have my own plans for Armageddon and don't always take the painkillers, secreting a small stockpile over the week in my bedside drawer, just in case.

The pain becomes literally unbearable, and sometimes I feel like my body is so inflamed and out of control that I might spontaneously combust.

We haven't got as far as tackling food concerns yet. Mum and Dad know not to push things too far. But we've started the exercise regime, and from my bed I raise and lower my arms, sometimes more than once, give a suggestion of pointing my feet like a plucky centurion ballerina with Alzheimer's, and even lift my head off the pillow now and again. Farcically, I feel worse each time but carry on so we can tick at least one of the boxes. Not so much tiny steps as microscopic ones.

I cry a lot and get easily angry. Dad christens me Linda after the girl actress in the Exorcist.

Don't call her that, Mum says, and he whispers, okay Ellen, (after the actress playing her mother in the film) so only I can hear him.

Mostly I'm left alone, festering, and raging in spurts in my head, my body hurting all over as if I'm being continuously tortured.

A pincer movement is coming together. The next day, I receive a note from Katherine, my counsellor. She normally visits the house but now she'd like to see me at the surgery. She knows how difficult this will be for me, as I haven't left the house in months. So, why is she asking me now?

Mum comes into my room with a new sheepskin cover for my wheelchair.

You'll need this, it's bitter out there.

I'm not bitter!

It's a nice one; you'll feel more comfortable.

Whoopee.

Hannah, please, I know it's hard for you, but Katherine may be able to help.

Well, she's not helping by making me come to the surgery.

I know, I'm not sure why –

Maybe it's a trap, and the social services will be hiding behind a door, waiting to take me away?

No, I don't think so.

You don't seem to care.

And Mum suddenly starts crying, and says, I do care, of course I care, I just don't know what's best anymore.

Stop crying, Mum, it's me who's ill.

And you don't think that affects me or your father?

God, I know it does.

Shall I help you get dressed?

Yes, please!

I'll get a brush; your hair is like a bird's nest.

Charming.

You have lovely hair, Hannah, you're lucky.

No-one has called me lucky in a long time.

Sorry –

No, I like it, don't stop.

Dad wheels me into the surgery and parks me in the waiting room. The dragon at reception has a form waiting. As Dad fills it in, she glares at me, a mixture of disdain and disapproval, and I think about sticking out my tongue, but I don't want to appear crazy to the other waiting patients.

A half-dead old man stares at me, shakes his head, and mouths 'sorry'.

Katherine's room is surprisingly bare. I'd fantasised a leather Freud couch, Persian rugs and portraits of crazed patients from an asylum along the wall. Instead, there are two red plastic chairs in the centre of the room, a stack of files and a small picture of two young children on her desk.

This is a borrowed room; sorry it's so austere.

Yours? I ask, pointing at the picture.

Yes, I bring the picture with me everywhere. Hopefully it helps soften things.

How old are they?

Six and seven. Now, how are you?

What are their names?

Hannah, how are you?

I didn't know you had children.

Hannah?

I feel terrible. The doctors have put me on an exercise regime and cut my painkillers.

Is it helping?

I said I feel terrible, didn't I?

You seem angry.

Do I?

How are you feeling?

Like shit.

I never normally swear with Katherine, but she looks calm in response, gives nothing away.

What does 'shit' mean for you? she asks.

I laugh. Sorry, it sounds funny the way you say it.

That's okay. How is the new dose of anti-depressants suiting you?

You know about that?

Are they helping?

Are you sharing information with the doctors?

No, everything we say in here stays between us.

I don't believe you.

Hannah, I'm telling you the truth.

Do you know how difficult it was for me to get out of bed and come here?

Yes, I do, and I'm very pleased that you came.

Pleased? It sounds like you're thanking me for coming to your seventh birthday party.

I know it was a big effort.

Do you believe I'm ill?

Of course, I know how terrible you feel.

That sounds ambiguous to me. Do you believe I'm physically ill or do you think it's somehow all in my mind?

Hannah, this isn't helping.

You won't answer?

It's what you think that matters. Not me.

And I scream as loud as I can and won't stop.

Dad comes panicking into the room.

As he wheels me out, still screaming, Katherine's features give nothing away, until she swallows and her neck bulges.

Dad wheels me through the waiting room and everyone stares. The sympathetic old man is tutting now, and I daren't even glance towards the reception desk.

The 'counselling debacle' (Dad's phrase for it) wiped me out and shredded my tonsils. Now I can't scream even if I want to, and my voice has become evil and gravelly just like the girl in The Exorcist.

From now on I'll only be prepared to feel worse after doing something I actually want to do. Like . . . God, I can't even think what that might be anymore.

Tinny pellet sounds tap-tap against my bedroom window, as if rice is being tossed at the pane. It comes in waves. Eventually, I turn on my bedside light, crawl out of bed and open the curtains a little. The moon is full, and someone is standing in our back garden. Yasmine! She gestures for me to open the window. When I do, she talks loud enough – but not shouting in case she wakes anyone – so I can hear:

Why won't you speak to me when I ring up?

I shrug my shoulders.

Still cross with me?

Go away!

No, I don't think I will. And what's with the voice?

How's Spike?

She laughs and comes closer to stand directly under the window, so it's less of a strain for my voice: De-spiked. Didn't Sarah tell you?

No, I haven't seen her for ages.

Can I come and see you soon?

I shake my head.

I promise I won't tire you out.

Maybe, but I need to go back to bed now.

Your new voice is sexy by the way, she says and blows a kiss up to me.

My performance at the surgery has had repercussions. Another letter from the medical team arrives – this time with a starker warning about non-co-operation – along with one from Social Services, who announce that they'll be visiting us next week 'as a matter of urgency'.

They're closing in, aren't they, Dad?

We'll be okay. You, Mum and I know what's best for you; we just need them to understand too.

You know you can make a bomb out of fertilizer, Dad.

I've told you before, Hannah, that kind of joke isn't funny.

Or we could drink lemonade laced with strychnine?

Like Jonestown, you mean? For your information, they drank Kool-Aid and added cyanide, not strychnine.

You've been thinking about it then?

And Dad gives me an unusually stern look, so I know not to continue.

Part of my parents' response to crises is to take back control, and they persuade me to go to my first M.E. group meeting.

Mum dresses me up in my Top Shop jean skirt – once a favourite, now way too big for me – and a new mohair jumper – way too prickly. She even plasters on some bronze foundation and persuades me to apply a film of red lipstick.

There, you look lovely, Hannah.

It's not a dating agency, Mum.

No, but you might meet someone nice.

She hands me a mirror: God, I look ridiculous.

Just rub a little of the foundation off.

Can you dampen a flannel for me, then?

She comes back with one and I rub the makeup away.

There you go, they get me warts and all, or not at all.

In the mirror, a pale ghost of a girl with sunken eyes and red scratched cheeks stares at me.

Well, maybe I could use a little on the cheeks then, but not like I'm auditioning to join the circus.

Circus is about right though when Dad wheels me into a church hall. It's done out like a Women's Guild fete, bunting, preserves and Tupperware on picnic tables, a flattering soft-focus portrait of the Queen above the stage. Grown-ups in a variety of M&S leisurewear are congregated at the back, and a circle of wheelchairs positioned at the front. I hear someone sobbing as a man drones on from the stage, something about care packages and benefits. Our arrival has been noticed and a vicious looking old bag in a tweed skirt comes to greet us – her name badge telling us she's 'Doreen'.

This must be your little Hannah, she says, looking at Dad.

You can talk to her, she understands everything, Dad tells her.

She bends down close to my face and smiles: Now, dear, we're going to get your father to park you by a lovely girl called Susan, though she likes to be called Suzie. She's a little older than you and isn't feeling well, either.

Thank you, Doreen, I say.

My use of her name wrong-foots her, and she eyes me with a look that labels me 'Trouble'.

I click my fingers. Off we go, James, I tell Dad, and he pushes my wheelchair next to Suzie's.

Ooh, she has the funky sheepskin cover too, I mutter under my breath.

I'll wait at the back, says Dad, and he applies the brake on my wheelchair.

I'm glad he did that; I might have got out onto the motorway and made my escape.

I'm Suzie, the girl says, and parents always do that, it helps them feel that they're protecting us.

I like the way you're thinking.

And I heard what you said about my 'funky' seat cover.

Oh.

It's okay; I hate mine too.

I like her already.

How long have you been ill? I ask her.

Five years.

Oh, I've only been ill a year.

I wouldn't say 'only'.

Is this your first meeting too, Suzie?

No, I come every month unless I'm having a bad relapse. My parents insist and Doreen is my grandmother.

She seems nice.

She isn't.

Is it helpful coming though?

No, I hate every minute.

Right.

What's your name?

Hannah.

Look, Hannah, it's all crap, and it'll never get better. But I have a way to put an end to it.

What do you mean?

Hannah, you mustn't tell anyone but I'm planning to kill myself.

She says it so flatly, matter-of-factly, and we don't speak again.

I sink back into my chair as another speaker on the stage waffles on – 'the importance of knowing your body and listening to what it's saying'.

Mine is quietly screaming. At the tea break, I tell Dad I feel ill and need to leave.

How was Suzie? he asks in the car.

She's nice.

Glad to hear it. The old lady said something strange about her, and Dad perfects her needling voice just right: 'Suzie is a good girl, but she has a very vivid imagination.'

Good old Doreen.

Bit of an old bag, eh? Well, perhaps you and Suzie could meet up sometime?

Don't think so, Dad.

Social Services were due to visit tomorrow but Mum and Dad have managed to put them off until next week. The medical assessment team have written again though, saying we must report to the surgery in a few days so they can monitor my progress with the exercise regime, weigh me, and assess the effects of the withdrawal of painkillers and higher doses of anti-depressants.

Another plan is needed and so Mum contacts an old friend who works for the local paper – The Snooper's Gazette, Dad likes to call it.

Mum's friend can't cover the story – 'conflict of interest' apparently – so Adrian, a trainee journalist arrives the next day.

I hear Dad explaining things to him in the hall: she's very ill but the doctors don't seem to understand and are imposing treatments on her that could make her worse.

They're even threatening to take her away if we don't comply, adds Mum.

We don't know that for sure, says Dad, but their tone is threatening. The worst thing is they don't listen.

Can I see Anna? Adrian asks.

It's Hannah, and yes you can but not for long.

I'll only ask a couple of questions, and maybe take a photo or two.

Three knocks on my door. Adrian would like to interview you now, Hannah, says Mum.

If you're up to it, Anna? Nothing quite as grand as an interview though, Adrian adds.

Come in, Adam, and my name is Hannah, starting and ending with 'h',

He doesn't get it.

What are your symptoms like? Is it like flu?

A bit like bad flu, I suppose.

A temperature?

No, it's more about deep aching, muscle pain, extreme exhaustion.

You get tired then?

More than tired.

More than tired, he repeats.

Jesus, Adrian's the type who says words as he writes them.

Do you want a photo?

It usually helps. You can take a moment to brush your hair if you like.

Thank you, but I'm fine.

Shall we put something on the –

I think 'commode' is the word you're looking for. But no, it's fine with me. Crop the photo if you must but I'd rather it stays. It's more honest.

He takes two photos. The first is of me looking suitably sad. The second is of me sarcastically smiling after he asked me to smile, 'because it'll make you look prettier'.

The car crash interview was completed just in time to make Friday's issue. First thing in the morning, Mum rushes to the newsagents for a copy. My article is on page seven, their human-interest section, next to the story of a pensioner whose had his mobility scooter jazzed up to look like a Harley Davidson motorbike. My sarcastic smile picture has been jettisoned for the sad smile picture, complete with sad commode. I look frightening, a ghostly white doll. Maybe a smile wasn't such a bad idea?

The headline is 'Flu Like Virus Leaves Anna, aged 15, in bed for a year'. At least he got my age right, but Adrian seems obsessed by the flu analogy and predictably also refers to M.E. as 'yuppie flu'. He goes on to say how Mum and Dad are taking on the authorities to 'stop any treatment'. Sounds like they want the drip taken down and my life support machine turned off. The article is a disaster, and Mum and Dad seem defeated by it. We barely speak for the rest of the day.

The paper comes out twice weekly and the next issue brings an unexpected deluge of letters in response to the article – well, three, which take up the whole of the letters section. One calls me 'tragic', another wonders what kind of 'rotten parents would allow a commode so close to a child's bed, 'and what's more, to allow it to be photographed so close to a child's bed'. None of us is sure what Mister G. Wilson's angle is here.

The last letter is the worst though. It calls my parents 'irresponsible' for challenging the medical professionals and goes on to say that 'their actions are putting a child in danger, and that something should be done about it!'

The leader article, normally consigned to rants about dog poo not being picked up or sex classes in schools, really puts the boot in. Their headline reads: 'How Childhoods Go Missing When Parents Stop Parenting'. None of us get past the first paragraph.

Tomorrow is my appointment at the surgery, and two days later Social Services will be arriving. I'm starting to wonder if I've saved enough of the painkillers to go round.

I look in the drawer, but they're gone.

Mum!

What? What? she says rushing in.

The pills, where are they?

Hannah, it's okay.

No!!!!

Don't scream, please! We've been reading and researching on the web, and we think there's something else you could take that will help with the pain, and it might make you feel a bit better too.

Heroin?

Not quite.

She opens her right hand to reveal a small black lump on a torn piece of tin foil.

What the hell is that?

It's something your Dad and I used to enjoy in the old days.

You're not serious –

Your Dad had to go to that dodgy pub behind the bus station to get this.

The old devil.

Less of 'the old', Dad says, coming in to join us.

I can't smoke though.

Just this once; I know it might make you feel awful at first but the effects once they hit, might be worth it? says Mum.

Don't knock something until you've tried it, Hannah, adds Dad.

It'll be okay, we'll take it with you, says Mum.

God, Mr G. Wilson was right when he called you 'rotten parents'.

Mum and Dad look startled.

Too much? I ask.

Too much, they say together, and we all laugh.

Once I stop coughing, I feel like my body is muffled, wrapped up in cotton wool, and whilst I'm trying to examine and describe this feeling, I notice something else, something missing. For this moment – and I don't know how long it'll last, but I stop myself questioning too much and instead try and relax – I'm not in agony. Yes, my lungs hurt a little, and my body feels slow and heavy but it's also free, free of pain.

Mum and Dad are in my room, sitting on the end of my bed. Dad sings along to Bob Dylan's 'Like A Rolling Stone', which he has blasting from the lounge.

Did I ever tell you that your Mum and I saw him, Hannah?

Only a thousand times, Dad.

Only a thousand times – God, Dad is talking so slowly – I thought I'd have told you more times than that.

You're so stupid, Mum says ruffling his hair. They kiss and it turns into a snog.

Ooh, get a room, I shout.

They smile soppily back at me.

There's tapping on my window, like grains of rice being tossed up against it again.

Someone must think you're getting married, I say, getting up and pulling open the curtains.

Yasmine beams up at me from the centre of the garden and curtsies, a giant love heart of rocks from the rockery shaped around her.

I wave at her to join us.

Wow, the Marrakesh Express, she says as she enters the fog of smoke enveloping my room.

She's soon taking a hit.

Very nice, she says. Lebanese?

Dad grins and gives the thumbs up.

Now his behaviour is way too weird to be embarrassing.

Heh, Yasmine do you know a Mr. G. Wilson of this Parish? asks Mum, as if she's turned into someone else.

No, I don't think so.

Mum stifles a giggle and continues: Mr. G. Wilson has a thing about commodes in bedrooms. Maybe thinks they should be in the toilet.

Bathroom, Dad corrects and snorts.

But if it was in the toilet, I mean bathroom, then it wouldn't be needed because you could just go the toilet.

A pause while we digest her logic.

And now we really are laughing, so hard I can barely catch my breath.

God, I'm hungry, I say.

Ah, takeaway time at last! Mum says. Curry or pizza or fish and chips?

Fish and Chips! Yasmine and I shout together.

Fish and chips it shall be, says Dad.

I'm going to pay for this but who cares, I think to myself.

Somehow, Yasmine reads my thoughts and holds me close: you'll be fine, Hannah.

When Dad leaves to get the takeaway, Mum stays seated on the lid of the commode; eyes closed, humming the Dylan song.

Hope your Mum is not about to use that, says Yasmine, gesturing at the commode. And who is this Mr. G. Wilson anyway?

Shush, Yas, we haven't got long left.

She climbs into bed with me, and for a moment everything feels possible.

Two Poems
Mary O'Donnell

The Walls of the Heart show Graffiti

With several breaks in one lifetime,
it somehow glued itself together, beat on

without surgeon's catgut, or artist's gold-leaf
sealing the damage, just basic grade red scarring,

twisted to bind. The sacks of its chambers
whisper, fill with sibilant utterance.

Scales offer a weighing up, interpretations:
Self against Self, proclaims the hoarding, one scale

muscling in on what's concealed—beads of desire,
shame, some bitter tears. The other scale

attempts to balance, presents a Janus head.
It gazes both ways, cool, rational, ignoring time.

Now, a reckoning, the tasking of heart to read
the scrawled inscriptions on its walls.

Despite whispers, it beats mercurially,
butterfly wings on a cold day, holds, then slows

to translate the passageways of blood, breaking rhythm to
accommodate a surge: graffiti,

sewer words, slang, then high, ancient language.
Babelonian and multiple, the tongues bleed easily

into valves and chambers, where life
writes an unsprung story, worn invisibly,
                              too lately understood.

Tenderness

It is here, when blood is a galaxy—spiral, elliptical
or irregular—carrying cells where their main business lies,
soft-washing heart and lungs, valves and bronchi,
and life continues in macro and micro.
It is there also when the broken post from which wisteria
swooned in spring purple, splinters and sags,

unable to bear the sinewy mother plant
beneath the soaking damp of winter.
We feel that weight as shared, because we know
what it is to have blossoms die, to limp on without welcome.
Tenderness, so ordinary it is not observed, is dirt beneath
our fingernails on an unwashed restaurant table,

it's the fallen pelvic muscle, or an off-course asteroid,
both threatening disaster, or breasts inclined to gravity
that still look to Jupiter's moons—Ganymede, Io—
for solace. Tenderness too, in the bitten tongue,
restrained as the tongue of the other
is unloosed and waggles without mercy,

or faith in silence. The traces of tenderness are scarcely
felt. It moves in us if allowed, like a breath
shared, it is a bird-saturated orchard watched carefully
in childhood through a morning window, now flowering
in your lungs like a forest, it describes also
how the child you never thought you'd have,

arrived capably from the cosmos one January,
a freight of tenderness, eagle in spirit.
Traces of a time and place in which everything was,
is, will be understood. The virtue is knowing no division
between bodies, bloods, galaxies in harmony
or disharmony   here   there   and within.

Two Poems for

Christopher Cornwell

Early Doors
(after John James)
John Goodby

But is the
earth as full as life was full, of them?
- 'A Step Away from Them', Frank O'Hara

A chill wet spring
this year

& the hanging gardens of Sketty
still ivy & bay

but then we still recall
the fens of Cambridgeshire

elaborate existences
on Catherine Street

those ubers summoned
for Rhydds Noah's Whitez

& on to the sunlit Uplands
always awaiting

deckled blue & gold
in ancient livery

& always too that view
of Mumbles Head in the distance

Ali & James Tian & Margaret weigh
a poem of the torn frenulum

& we jest about Urquhart's Rabelais
in the gloom of the New Brunswick

your fuliginous black beard
& greatcoat gravitas of a Titian prince

that will suddenly gaudy & out
Omar Pasha by Ashley Bickerton

wit ever gleaming sharp-shiny
as Ade's arrows in The Railway Inn

a kind prodigious intelligence
to seek love & find it finally

though by then the rain had come down
on certain forlorn dark nights

not doucement doucement no
but filthy off the Celtic Sea

now a rural allotmenteer
before work I raise my Corbyn mug

cherishing your potlatch gift
to be unsparing & yet generous

and *The Accursed Share*
with its Missing you already, my friend

sorrow as the clock ticks past six
but knowing not your words did this

or any armful of gritty leeks
ergasy inkhorn or aureate

& that they speak true poesy
as you to our hearts cerebral cerebral

so mix me a special with ice in the kitchen
so set me a place at your Sunday roast

& from Brynmill to Burwell
register surf-noise at the sea's lip

cheep of marsh-water running clear
& lark & gull above either

corny & true as you would know
who were so ahead of us all

& being in with the flow
to return as amused reason must

to smile & quiz
& leave us in your wake to learn

dear interlocutor dear flit
Chris you're away & up for it

Incomplete Text
John Lavin

'Brilliance is a category of exclusion as much as any other abnormality' –
Christopher Cornwell

I don't complete poems very often – and never quickly –
So please forgive me for writing in haste
And for writing *this* kind of thing
The sort of blank heart-on-the-sleeve verse
That you hated
That you would hardly countenance
Writing yourself
'If poetry relies on simple mainstream language,
It withers and diminishes'
You once wrote in this very magazine, before adding:
'Language must become non-normative. Become extraordinary.'

Speaking of language, the penultimate time I messaged you
You said you weren't sure if you would write poetry again

You seemed to lose some of your passion for composition
Not long after *Ergasy* was published
Did I contribute to that?
Did I hinder more than help, publishing your book?

I have worried about that but I know it to be a concern that says
more about my own self-absorption than anything tangibly relating
to your psyche

And yet

Yes

I think that after the initial sense of achievement you were left with a
perfectly-realised document of your despair
I remember you saying that you had to remove sections from the
book before you could give a copy to your grandmother and it was
obvious that that wasn't something to raise my eyebrows about, the
way one might do fondly about an elderly relative too sensitive to
deal with certain subject matter
No, it was a wound from long ago
A wound roughly re-opened
A wound such as would never heal
An attitude so foreign to your brilliance
That it shouldn't have been able to hurt you
But beauty and truth aren't the shield we both once thought they
might be
And the ceremony of innocence, as we know, is daily drowned anew

You told me about those last minute excisions from *Ergasy* late at
night in the summer of 2019
Greg was asleep beside you and Michou – in her third trimester with
Aldous – long gone upstairs
We were talking more directly than usual and now I think of it I was
in a strung out mood myself, anxious about impending fatherhood
and stricken by my own father's late-period dementia
As a result I was unusually direct with you, whereas I would usually
demure, sensing you didn't like to be cornered
I wish I had been that direct with you more often

I can't remember exactly but it might be that you only removed the
pages in the garden when you finally got to Frinton-on-Sea
Perhaps you had been in two minds
Faraway lonely Frinton where you walked your grandmother's
geriatric Alsatian along the clifftops and read book after book after
book
A place my parents had visited once in the 70s before being asked to
stop picnicking on the green
'Well, that's very Frinton,' I remember you saying through pursed
lips where I had expected to elicit a smile

That night in 2019 we embraced on the landing for what felt like a
long time
It's not how I'll remember you the most
Because I'll remember your kindness and wit
Your laughter and poetry and friendship best of all
But you were like a damaged building
Your integrity severely undermined
And I felt like I was holding you up

Maybe that was the closest I'd ever felt to understanding what is was
to be you
Maybe there is a part of us that will always be innocent, that will
always be a helpless child in a room full of adults
You kept that part of yourself well hidden – at least from me –
But I saw you then, faraway and lonely in some far distant past, and I
didn't know what to say
Except
'Love you, Chris'
At least I think I said something to that effect
I hope I'm not misremembering that

I suppose it's obvious upon reflection that *Ergasy* was such a
summation of your being at that point in time that having to excise
certain sections for someone whose opinion you valued so deeply
was akin to an act of serious self-harm
When I messaged you about Issue Fourteen you said you had no new
poems and you didn't know if you'd write again
Perhaps because you had finally found happiness in a relationship
you no longer felt the need and perhaps poetry felt too decadent,
maybe it struck your burgeoning social conscience as something
unnecessarily dilettantish in a world of terrible injustice
Nevertheless, I couldn't understand it either then or now because
you were as close to being a poetic genius as anyone I've ever met
and maybe that's because
Writing is so important to me
That I treat it like a God I'm not worthy of

You weren't like that
You were like a poet from another age
You were completely uninterested in literary fashions and trends
Something which can be dull in others because it is either a deliberate
untruth or a reflection of a closed worldview
But you were a genuine intellectual, one of the few literary ones I've
ever met
You had it within you to forge the zeitgeist so why would you worry
about people that pretend to
To be a true poet is to be the opposite of someone in search of
relevance
To be the opposite of someone in search of a career
I won't say the opposite of someone in search of acceptance
Because I think deep down you were always looking for that
And I think a true poet writes to be accepted on their own terms

And that was always you, always dear sweet you
Always asking to be accepted on your own terms

Authors in Order of Appearance

Medbh McGuckian was born in 1950 in Belfast where she continues to live. She has been Writer-in-Residence at Queen's University, Belfast, the University of Ulster, Coleraine, and Trinity College, Dublin, and was Visiting Fellow at the University of California, Berkeley. She is Honorary Lecturer at Queen's University's School of Arts, English and Languages Department.

Her books (published by the Gallery Press) include *Venus and the Rain, On Ballycastle Beach, Marconi's Cottage, Captain Lavender, The Flower Master & Other Poems, Selected Poems, Shelmalier, Drawing Ballerinas, The Face of the Earth, Had I A Thousand Lives, The Book of the Angel, The Currach Requires No Harbours, My Love has Fared Inland, The High Caul Cap, Blaris Moor, Marine Cloud Brightening* and *The Thankless Paths to Freedom.*

Among the prizes she has won are England's National Poetry Competition, the Cheltenham Award, the Rooney Prize, the Bass Ireland Award for Literature, the Denis Devlin Award, the Alice Hunt Bartlett Prize, and, in 2002, the Forward Prize for Best Poem. She received the American Ireland Fund Literary Award in 1998 and an honorary Doctorate from the University of Aberdeen. Medbh McGuckian is a member of Aosdána.

Mary Morrissy is an award-winning Irish novelist (The Hennessy Award, Lannan Foundation Award) and short story writer, the author of four novels, *Mother of Pearl, The Pretender, The Rising of Bella Casey* and *Penelope Unbound,* as well as two collections of short stories, *A Lazy Eye* and *Prosperity Drive.*

John Goodby is Professor of Arts and Culture at Sheffield Hallam University. He is a poet, critic, and translator, and an authority on Dylan Thomas, whose *Collected Poems* he edited in 2014. His poetry books include *Illennium* (Shearsman, 2010) and *The No Breath* (Red Ceilings, 2017), and he has published translations of Soleiman Adel Guemar (with Tom Cheesman), Heine, Pasolini and Reverdy. With Lyndon Davies he ran the Hay Poetry Jamborees 2009-12 and edited the anthology *The Edge of Necessary: innovative Welsh poetry 1966-2018* (Aquifer, 2018). His edition of the lost fifth notebook of Dylan Thomas, edited with Ade Osbourne, is published by Bloomsbury. His latest chapbook of poems is *So, Rise* (Red Ceilings Press).

Taz Rahman was shortlisted for the 2022 Aesthetica Creative Writing Prize and his first poetry collection was published by Seren Books in February 2024. His poems have appeared in numerous issues of *Poetry Wales, Bad Lilies, Anthropocene, Propel, Honest Ulsterman* and *South Bank Poetry*. He is the founder of the Books Council of Wales supported You Tube poetry channel Just Another Poet.

Emily Devane is a writer, editor, bookseller and teacher based in Ilkley, West Yorkshire. She has taught workshops and courses for Comma Press, Dahlia Press, London Writers' Café and Northern Writers' Studio. She has won the Bath Flash Fiction Award, a Northern Writers' Award and a Word Factory Apprenticeship. Emily's work has been published in *Smokelong Quarterly* (third place, Grand Micro Contest 2021), *Best Microfictions Anthology* (2021), *New Flash Fiction Review, Lost Balloon, Ellipsis, New Flash Fiction Review, Janus Literary, Ambit* and others. She was a BIFFY50 editor in 2020 and is a founding editor at *FlashBack Fiction*. Emily co-hosts Word Factory's Strike! Short Story Club. She was shortlisted for the prestigious Mogford Prize for Food and Drink Writing, and she also won second place in the Bath

Short Story Award. She judged the October 2022 round of the Bath Flash Fiction Award.

Breda Spaight's work has appeared in *The Lonely Crowd, Poetry Ireland, Southword, The Stinging Fly, Ambit, Aesthetica,* and others. Her debut chapbook, *The Untimely Death of My Mother's Hens,* is published by Southword Editions in the New Irish Voices Series. Her debut collection is forthcoming from Arlen House. She is the recipient of an Arts Council of Ireland Literature Bursary.

Fiona O'Connor is a Hennessy Award winner and Francis MacManus Award finalist. She contributes to the *Irish Times* and reviews for the *Morning Star.* She is published in anthologies such as *Sublunary Editions, Stinging Fly, Fiction International,* and *The Lonely Crowd.*

Poet, critic, essayist, expert on Welsh Art, **Tony Curtis** was born in Carmarthen in West Wales in 1946. He studied at Swansea University and Goddard College, Vermont. He is the author of numerous collections of poetry, including *From the Fortunate Isles: New and Selected Poems.* He has also written volumes of critical work on poets and artists and edited popular anthologies of poetry. He is Emeritus Professor of Poetry at the University of South Wales, where he established and was Director of the MPhil in Writing for many years. He has been elected to the Royal Society of Literature and has toured widely reading his poetry to international audiences.

Conor Montague is from Galway, in the west of Ireland. Currently based in London, Conor facilitates workshops for London Writers Eclective and is resident playwright at the Irish Cultural Centre, Hammersmith.

His fiction has been placed/shortlisted for The Bridport Prize, the V.S. Pritchett Award, Fish Prize, the Bath Flash Fiction Award, The

Writers Bureau Flash Fiction Comp, Hammond House International Literary Prize, Oxford Flash Fiction Prize and Reflex Flash Fiction Comp. Conor's debut collection of short fiction, *Capital Vices*, was published by Reflex Press in Autumn 2023.

Hilary Watson lives in Cardiff. She's a graduate of Warwick University's Writers' Programme and was a Jerwood/Arvon Mentee 2015/16 with mentor Caroline Bird. She has been shortlisted for the Troubadour International Poetry Prize and the York Poetry Prize, and recently been published in Poetry Wales, Pomegranate London and Magma.

Catherine Wilkinson was first published in *The Lonely Crowd*'s Issue 11: 'Grey Wizard' is also in audio form on www.thelonelycrowd.org. Introduced as 'an exquisite painterly story concerning a horse', it also lingers lightly upon art and chromesthesia. In Issue 13, she acted as guest editor for the non-fiction section and contributed two interviews with the acclaimed authors, Horatio Clare and Cynan Jones. The on-line lit magazine, *Storgy*, has published other stories by Wilkinson - including 'Exeat', set in Berlin, the first episode of the singular man-boy Ludo featured in this issue's 'Intermission'. Longer work includes *Island Journal* (2018) and her current fiction works in progress, *Botanicum* and *Petitgrain*.

Linda McKenna's debut poetry collection, *In the Museum of Misremembered Things*, was published by Doire Press in 2020. The title poem won the An Post/Irish Book Awards, Irish Poem of the Year. In 2018 she won the Seamus Heaney Award for New Writing and the Red Line Festival Award. She has had poems published in a variety of publications including, *Poetry Ireland Review, Banshee, The North, The Honest Ulsterman, Crannóg, Atrium, The Poetry Bus, One, Abridged, The Stony Thursday Book.*

Cath Barton is an English writer who lives in South Wales. Her published novellas are *The Plankton Collector* (2018, New Welsh Review), *In the Sweep of the Bay* (2020, Louise Walters Books) and *Between the Virgin and the Sea* (2023, Novella Express, Leamington Books). She has a fourth novella, *The Geography of the Heart*, forthcoming from Arroyo Seco Press. A pamphlet of her short stories, *Mr Bosch and His Owls*, is due to be published by Atomic Bohemian in 2024.

Jackie Gorman is from the midlands of Ireland. Her poetry has been published in a number of journals including *Poetry Ireland Review* and *The Honest Ulsterman*. She received the Listowel Writers' Week Single Poem Award in 2017 and in the same year was commended in the Bord Gais Energy Irish Book Awards Poem of the Year Award and was part of the Poetry Ireland Introductions Series. She has a MA in Poetry Studies from DCU. Her debut collection *The Wounded Stork* was published in 2019 by The Onslaught Press and was described by Martin Dyar as 'an engrossing and ecologically attuned debut.' She recently featured in the Ireland Chair of Poetry Anthology *Hold Open The Door*, published by UCD Press. In 2021, she received an Agility Award from the Arts Council of Ireland.

Órfhlaith Foyle is a short story writer, poet and dramatist and lives in Galway. She's published a novel, a poetry collection and two volumes of short stories. She also wrote and directed the radio dramas *May's End* and *How I Murdered Lucrezia*, which were both adapted from her short stories and received full BAI funding, as well as premiering on Newstalk Radio.

'A Letter of Sorts to Dylan Thomas' was originally published in her latest short story collection, *Three Houses in Rome* (Doire Press).

Pauline Flynn is an Irish Visual Artist/Poet. She was shortlisted for the Patrick Kavanagh Poetry Award in 2010. Published in — *Poetry Ireland Review, Eavan Boland Special Issue, 2022, Skylight 47, Boyne Berries, Sixteen Magazine, Into the Light, Orbis 81, Light, a Journal of Photography and Poetry, Silver Birch Press, The Blue Nib.* She lives in Co. Wicklow.

Karys Frank is the winner of the 2023 Lindisfarne Prize for Crime Fiction. Her short stories have been published in Mslexia, by Retreat West Books and also by Otranto House Books. Frank is also the recipient of a Northern Writers' New Fiction award from New Writing North.

Jane Lovell lives in North Devon on the edge of the Valley of Rocks. Her work focuses on our relationship with the planet and its wildlife. She has recently won the Ginkgo Prize and the Rialto Nature & Place Poetry Competition. Her new collection, *On Earth, as it is,* is published by Hazel Press.

As well as *The Lonely Crowd,* **Lucie McKnight Hardy's** stories have featured in a variety of publications, including *Best British Short Stories 2019, Uncertainties IV, The New Abject, Black Static* and as a limited edition chapbook from Nightjar Press.

Her debut novel, *Water Shall Refuse Them,* was published by Dead Ink Books in 2019. Of her second book, *Dead Relatives,* the Guardian said, 'This short story collection confirms the author's reputation in the field of literary horror.'

Novelist, poet, photographer, essayist and short story writer, **Jo Mazelis** grew up in Swansea, later living in Aberystwyth and then London for over 14 years before returning to her hometown. Her novel *Significance* was awarded the Jerwood Fiction Uncovered Prize 2015. Her first collection of short stories *Diving Girls* was shortlisted for both Wales Book of the Year and Commonwealth Best First Book. Her book *Circle Games* was long-listed for Wales Book of the Year. Her third collection of stories *Ritual, 1969* was long-listed for the Edge Hill Prize and shortlisted for Wales Book of the Year in 2017. *Blister and Other Stories* was shortlisted for the Rubery Award in 2023. She has taught creative writing for Swansea University's Department of Adult Continuing Education, at Trinity College, Carmarthen and for residential courses at the Arvon Foundation.

Her poems have appeared in *Abridged, The Lonely Crowd, Poetry Wales, New Welsh Review* and *Bad Lilies* among other places.

Angela Graham is from Belfast. She has had a successful career in Wales as a producer in TV and film. She now lives in Wales and N. Ireland. Her collection of poetry, *Sanctuary: There Must Be Somewhere* was published by Seren Books in 2022. Her short story collection *A City Burning* came out in 2020 and was longlisted for the Edge Hill Short Story Prize

Fiona Cameron teaches Creative Writing at Bangor University. She is the author of two poetry collections: *Bendigo* (Knives Forks and Spoons Press, 2015) and *She May Be Radon* (Knives Forks and Spoons Press, 2021) Recent creative work has appeared in *Poetry Wales, Strix, Horror Across Borders, The Ghastling* and *The New Welsh Review*. Forthcoming critical work examines the female experience of the supernatural in children's/YA fiction and TV of the 70s and 80s.

Alan McCormick lives in Wicklow. He's a trustee of InterAct Stroke Support who read fiction and poetry to stroke patients.

His writing has appeared in *The Stinging Fly, Southword, Banshee, Confingo, Popshot, Best British Short Stories, Sonder, Poetry Bus and Exacting Clam*; and online at *3:AM Magazine, Dead Drunk Dublin, Fictive Dream, Mono, Words for the Wild* and *Époque Press*. His story, 'Fire

Starter', came second in 2022's RTÉ Short Story Competition, and 'Boys On Film' was runner up in this year's Plaza Sudden Fiction Prize.

Mary O'Donnell's poetry collections include *Unlegendary Heroes, Those April Fevers* (Ark Publications) and *Massacre of the Birds* (Salmon Poetry). Four novels include *Where They Lie* (2014) and the best-selling debut novel *The Light Makers*, reissued in 2017 by 451 Editions. Her stories have been published by Stand Magazine, The Fiddlehead Review, The Manchester Review, The French Literary Review, the London Magazine, and in the anthology The Glass Shore. Her most recent collection of short stories, *Empire*, which focuses on social and family situations before, during and after the Irish Rising in 1916, was published by Arlen House. She won the Fish International Short Story Competition in 2010. Her essay 'My Mother in Drumlin Country' was published in New Hibernia Review and listed among the Notable Essays of 2017 in Best American Essays (Mariner). She is a member of Ireland's affiliation of artists, Aosdana. Her fifth novel is awaiting publication.

About the Editor

John Lavin has a doctorate in Creative Writing from the University of Wales, Trinity Saint David, as well as an MA in The Teaching and Practice of Creative Writing from Cardiff University. He is the founding Editor of *The Lonely Crowd*. He is also the former Fiction Editor of Wales Arts Review, and the editor of their short story anthologies, *A Fiction Map of Wales* and *Story: Retold*. He also co-founded – and for many years co-edited – the literary journal, *The Lampeter Review*. His criticism has appeared in *The Irish Times, Wales Arts Review, The Lampeter Review* and *The Welsh Agenda*.

*

Online Fiction Editor

We are delighted to have a new online fiction editor....

Matthew David Scott is a writer, editor and teacher based in Newport. His fiction has been listed for the Dylan Thomas Prize, the Rhys Davies Short Story Award, and he is a recipient of the Samuel Beckett Theatre Trust Award, with the theatre company he co-founded, Slung Low. He is on Instagram if you want to say hello: @matthew.david.scott